JANE AUSTEN'S

PRIDE&
PREJUDICE

A RETELLING BY LAURA WOOD

U

UNION
SQUARE
& CO.

NEW YORK

**UNION
SQUARE
& CO.**

NEW YORK

UNION SQUARE & CO. and the distinctive Union Square & Co. logo
are trademarks of Sterling Publishing Co., Inc.

Union Square & Co., LLC, is a subsidiary of Sterling Publishing Co., Inc.

Text © 2022 Laura Wood
Cover illustration © 2024 Helen Crawford-White

First published in Great Britain in 2022 by Barrington Stoke Ltd.
First published in the United States and Canada in 2024
by Union Square & Co., LLC.

ISBN 978-1-4549-5482-8

Library of Congress Control Number: 2023942894

For information about custom editions, special sales, and premium
purchases, please contact specialsales@unionsquareandco.com.

Printed in China

2 4 6 8 10 9 7 5 3 1

unionsquareandco.com

Union Square & Co.'s EVERYONE CAN BE A READER books are expertly
written, thoughtfully designed with dyslexia-friendly fonts and paper
tones, and carefully formatted to meet readers where they are with
engaging stories that encourage reading success across a wide range
of age and interest levels.

For my mum

1.

Mr. Bennet was not a man who gave out many compliments, but today he looked around him and thought—almost in surprise—that his girls made a pretty picture.

Jane, the eldest, was working at her embroidery, her gold hair shining in the light falling through the window. Kitty and Lydia, his two youngest daughters, were looking at a magazine that showed off the latest fashions, and Mary, the middle daughter, was reading, her face hidden in her book.

Elizabeth, his second oldest daughter and Mr. Bennet's particular favorite, was putting a new ribbon on her hat. Her dark eyes sparkled as she laughed at something that Jane said. Mr. Bennet was just about to ask Lizzy what the joke was when this peaceful scene was interrupted.

"My dear Mr. Bennet!" Mrs. Bennet cried, rushing into the room. "Have you heard the news? Netherfield Park has been let at last!"

Mr. Bennet said that he had not heard the news.

"Mrs. Long has just been here, and she told me all about it," Mrs. Bennet said, as if Mr. Bennet had not spoken.

This time Mr. Bennet made no answer at all and returned to reading his newspaper.

"Do you want to know *who* will be living there?" cried his wife impatiently.

"You want to tell me, and I have no objection to hearing it," Mr. Bennet said, lowering the paper with a sigh.

This was all the encouragement that Mrs. Bennet needed, and Lizzy Bennet bit her lip to keep from laughing.

"Mrs. Long says that a young man with a large fortune from the north of England came down on Monday to see the place, and he was so happy with it that he agreed to take it at once." Mrs. Bennet rocked back on her heels happily, her hands clasped to her chest.

"What is his name?" Jane asked.

"His name is Mr. Bingley." Mrs. Bennet said his name as if it were something quite delicious. "And he is not married!" she continued. "A single man with a large fortune—four or five thousand pounds a year. What a fine thing for our girls!"

2

Mr. Bennet looked puzzled. "Why is it a fine thing for our daughters?" he asked.

"My dear Mr. Bennet," his wife replied, looking at him as though he were a simpleton. "How can you be so tiresome? It will be a fine thing for our girls because he will *marry* one of them."

"Oh, is *that* why he is moving here?" Mr. Bennet raised his eyebrows.

"Because a single man in possession of a good fortune *must* be in want of a wife." Lizzy smiled.

"What nonsense you talk," Mrs. Bennet huffed. "Of course he is looking for a wife! And I am sure he will fall in love with one of our girls, and so Mr. Bennet *must* visit him as soon as he arrives."

"I see no need for that. You and the girls may go and visit him," Mr. Bennet said. "Or maybe you should send them alone, in case Mr. Bingley falls in love with *you* instead."

Kitty and Lydia began to giggle at that, but Mrs. Bennet did not seem to notice.

"When a woman has five grown-up daughters, she should not be thinking of her own beauty," Mrs. Bennet replied, but she couldn't help casting a quick glance at the mirror over the fireplace.

Mr. and Mrs. Bennet were indeed blessed with five daughters but a worrying lack of sons. This meant that when Mr. Bennet died, his estate would be passed on to his nearest male relative, and his wife and daughters would be left with very little indeed.

The matter of getting her daughters married therefore weighed heavily on Mrs. Bennet's mind.

It weighed on Mr. Bennet's mind as well, although he did not like to show it. Which is why he let his wife continue complaining that he was a cold and unfeeling man, while he made his own plans to visit Mr. Bingley as soon as possible.

Mr. Bennet smiled behind his newspaper. He did enjoy teasing his family.

2.

The Bennet family had been eagerly awaiting the ball at the assembly rooms the following week. It would be the first time that they would meet Mr. Bingley.

The assembly rooms in which the ball was held were split into three separate rooms: the ballroom, where there was music and couples danced; the card room, where card games were played and occasionally fortunes were won or lost; and the dining room, where refreshments were served. Everything looked splendid—a whirl of pretty dresses and happy faces lit by hundreds of candles.

Lizzy was with her sisters and mother in the ballroom when Mr. Bingley arrived with four other people—two women and two men.

"Those are Mr. Bingley's sisters," Mrs. Long, a friend of Mrs. Bennet, whispered. "And that man is Mr. Hurst, his sister's husband." She pointed to the older of the two men.

"Who is the other gentleman?" Mrs. Bennet asked. "He is very handsome."

"*That* is Mr. Darcy," Mrs. Long replied. "They say he has a fortune of ten thousand pounds a year!"

Lizzy overheard this. "I expect Mother thinks him even more handsome now," she whispered to Jane.

Mr. Bingley and his guests were very grand, dressed in the finest clothes. His sisters looked around with obvious disapproval—it seemed this ball was not up to their standards. Mr. Bingley was almost as handsome as Mr. Darcy, with curly blond hair and a wide smile that suggested *he* was very pleased with everything he saw, even if his sisters weren't.

This smile seemed to widen even further when Mr. Bingley's eyes rested on Jane. The two of them stared at each other for a few intense seconds, then Jane dropped her eyes and blushed.

Lizzy looked thoughtfully at Mr. Darcy. It was true that he was a very good-looking man. He was tall and dark-haired, with sharp cheekbones and dark eyes, but his expression was very serious and his dark eyes were cold.

Mr. Bingley wasted no time being introduced to everyone—he was lively and friendly, and danced every dance.

What a difference between him and his friend! Mr. Darcy danced only twice—once with Mrs. Hurst and once with Miss Bingley. He would not speak to any other lady and spent the evening ignoring everyone.

Soon the chatter at the ball was that Mr. Darcy was the proudest, most disagreeable man in the world.

But there was worse to come.

Lizzy had been forced to sit out two of the dances because there were fewer men than women at the ball. She heard a voice coming from nearby while sitting in her seat, watching the dancing. It was Mr. Bingley.

"Come on, Darcy," said Mr. Bingley. "You must dance."

"I certainly shall not," Mr. Darcy replied.

Lizzy sank lower in her chair so that they would not see her as she listened to their conversation.

"You know how I detest dancing unless I know my partner very well," Mr. Darcy went on. "Your sisters are busy, and there is not another woman in the room I would even consider dancing with."

"Upon my honor!" cried Mr. Bingley. "I never met so many pleasant girls in my life as I have this evening. Several of them are very pretty indeed."

"You have been dancing with the only handsome girl in the room," said Mr. Darcy, and Lizzy realized he was talking about Jane.

"Oh! She is the most beautiful creature I ever saw!" Mr. Bingley exclaimed. "But there is her sister Miss Elizabeth Bennet, who is very pretty, and I dare say very agreeable. Do let me ask my partner to introduce you."

Lizzy stiffened at hearing her name, not sure that she wanted anything to do with Mr. Darcy. He seemed to be a terrible snob.

"She is tolerable, but not handsome enough to tempt me," Mr. Darcy replied to Mr. Bingley. He spoke in a low voice, but not so low that Lizzy did not hear him.

Mr. Bingley left to dance with Jane again and Mr. Darcy wandered off, leaving Lizzy feeling no kindness toward him at all. However, it was not long before Lizzy began to chuckle to herself, and then she took great joy in sharing the story with her friends. She did a wonderful impression of

Mr. Darcy by sticking her nose up in the air and growling, "She is *tolerable*."

All in all it was a pleasant evening for the whole family. Mrs. Bennet had seen her eldest daughter much admired, and Mr. Bingley had danced with Jane *twice*!

Lizzy squeezed Jane's hand as they left, knowing that her shy, quiet sister was as excited as their mother in her own way. Jane gave Lizzy a dazzling smile.

Lizzy's other sisters were also happy. Mary had heard someone saying to Miss Bingley that she was the most accomplished girl in the neighborhood, while Kitty and Lydia had danced every dance. They returned, therefore, in good spirits to Longbourn, the village where they lived, and Mrs. Bennet recounted the story of the night's events to Mr. Bennet with glee.

3.

Later that night, Jane and Lizzy were finally alone. At last they could talk about the ball and—much more importantly—about Mr. Bingley.

"He is just what a young man should be," said Jane. "He's sensible, good-humored, lively—and I never saw such happy manners!"

"He is also handsome," replied Lizzy with a twinkle in her eye, "which a young man should be, if he possibly can."

"I was very surprised that he asked me to dance a second time," Jane said, lowering her eyes. "I did not expect such a compliment."

"Did you not?" Lizzy nudged her. "*I* did. Mr. Bingley certainly saw that you were about five times as pretty as every other woman in the room. Well, he is very nice, and I'm happy that you like him. You have liked many a stupider person."

"Lizzy!" Jane exclaimed.

"Oh, but it's true! You seem to find the good in everybody, Jane. I never heard you speak ill of a human being in your life." Lizzy laughed. "I suppose you even liked Mr. Bingley's sisters?"

"Not at first," Jane admitted, "but after I spoke to them for a while I thought them very nice. Miss Bingley is going to live with her brother, and I think she will be a charming neighbor for us."

Lizzy listened in silence but was not convinced. The girls had a lot to think about when they finally blew out the candle and went to sleep.

The next morning, the Bennets were visited by their neighbor Charlotte Lucas, the eldest daughter of Lord and Lady Lucas, and her young brother. Charlotte was a quiet, sensible young woman of twenty-seven, and a great friend of Lizzy. She too had attended the ball the previous night.

"You began the evening well, Charlotte," said Mrs. Bennet when they were all sitting down with cups of tea. "You were Mr. Bingley's first choice as a dance partner."

"Yes," Charlotte agreed, "but he seemed to like his second choice better."

"Oh! You mean Jane, because he danced with her twice," Mrs. Bennet said, her pleasure barely hidden.

"I overheard Mr. Bingley talking to another guest," Charlotte went on, her eyes dancing. "He said that he thought Jane was the prettiest young woman in the room."

"Well, that is very interesting!" Mrs. Bennet looked as if she might burst at this news.

"I think what I overheard was a lot more pleasant than what Lizzy overheard," said Charlotte. "Mr. Darcy is not so worth listening to as his friend, is he? Poor Lizzy, to be called only *tolerable*."

"I beg you not to talk about him," Mrs. Bennet huffed. "He is such a disagreeable man!"

"Miss Bingley told me," said Jane, "that Mr. Darcy never speaks much, unless among his close friends. With them he is very agreeable."

"I do not believe a word of it, my dear." Mrs. Bennet frowned. "And I hope that if he ever does ask you to dance, Lizzy, you will say no."

"I think I can safely promise *never* to dance with him," Lizzy said with a smile.

"If I were as rich as Mr. Darcy," interrupted Charlotte's young brother, "I would have a whole lot of dogs, and drink a bottle of wine every day."

"Then you would drink a great deal too much," said Mrs. Bennet, "and I would take the bottle away from you!"

The boy protested that she would not, she continued to say that she would, and the argument ended only when the visit was over and the Lucas family went home.

4.

For the next two weeks, Lizzy watched Jane's admiration for Mr. Bingley grow. It was in Jane's every smile, in every blush, in the light Lizzy saw in her sister's eyes.

"If Mr. Bingley does not realize that Jane is in love with him, then he is a fool," Lizzy said to her friend Charlotte Lucas one evening. The two girls were at a party held at Charlotte's family's house.

"But remember, Lizzy, Mr. Bingley does not know Jane as well as you do," Charlotte replied. "They always meet in large parties like this one where there is hardly any time for them to talk. If Jane wants him, she must make it clear."

Lizzy laughed, surprised at her friend's boldness, but Charlotte shook her head.

"I'm serious," Charlotte said.

Lizzy frowned. "They have only known each other for two weeks—it's too soon for Jane to know her own heart."

"Perhaps. But Mr. Bingley seems to be a kind man who will look after her." Charlotte sighed. "That may be all any of us can ask for."

Lizzy was silent. She knew that she had to get married one day, but she certainly hoped for more than the life Charlotte described.

"Come," Charlotte said, changing the subject. "I think it is time for you to entertain our guests." She patted the top of the piano. "Will you play and sing for us, Lizzy?"

Lizzy's piano playing was by no means perfect, but she played and sang with great emotion. The crowd at the party enjoyed her performance very much, but Lizzy felt the gaze of one gentleman in particular: Mr. Darcy.

Over the last two weeks, Mr. Darcy had found himself increasingly drawn to Miss Elizabeth Bennet. He liked her warm laughter and her dancing brown eyes. He had begun to wish to know her better, but he had no idea how to go about it.

After a song or two, Lizzy left the piano so that her sister Mary could play instead. Mary worked very hard at her piano practice—much harder than Lizzy—and she was always happy to show off her skills.

Mary played some complicated pieces but finally gave in to Lydia and Kitty. They were pleading for a song they could dance to.

Lord Lucas beckoned Lizzy over as he spoke to Mr. Darcy.

"What a charming amusement for young people this is, Mr. Darcy!" Lord Lucas said. "My dear Miss Bennet, why are you not dancing? Mr. Darcy, you must allow me to present this young lady to you as a very desirable partner." He took Lizzy's hand to give to Mr. Darcy, but she drew back.

"Indeed, sir, I have no intention of dancing," Lizzy said firmly.

"But I would be honored to have this dance," Mr. Darcy said with a bow.

Lizzy could tell that Mr. Darcy thought it should be impossible to refuse him.

"Mr. Darcy is all politeness," said Lizzy, smiling. "But I am afraid I will not be dancing this evening."

With this she turned away and went in search of Jane.

Mr. Darcy was surprised. When Miss Bingley found him several minutes later, he was frowning, deep in thought.

"I can guess what you are thinking," Miss Bingley said.

"I should imagine not," Mr. Darcy replied.

"You are thinking how awful it would be to have to spend many more evenings like this one. These people are terrible," Miss Bingley said, tucking her hand through his arm.

"You are wrong," Mr. Darcy said lightly. "I have been thinking about the very great pleasure which a pair of fine eyes in the face of a pretty woman can bestow."

Miss Bingley dropped his arm in surprise. "But who do you mean?" she asked breathlessly. "Whose eyes are you admiring?"

"Miss Elizabeth Bennet," Mr. Darcy replied.

5.

The days drifted by, and the following week a letter arrived for Jane. She opened it while the Bennet family were gathered around the breakfast table. It was from Caroline Bingley, Mr. Bingley's sister.

"She invites me to join her and her sister for dinner tonight," Jane said. Her happiness was clear, and matched by Mrs. Bennet, who clapped her hands in delight.

"Can I take the carriage?" Jane asked.

Mrs. Bennet looked out the window thoughtfully. "No, my dear, you had better go on horseback. It seems like it will rain, and then you will be invited to stay the night."

Jane protested that it would be very rude to impose herself in such a way, but her mother would not listen. Soon the whole family was standing by the front door waving Jane off as she rode away toward Netherfield Park, where Mr. Bingley and his guests were staying.

Hardly any time had passed when the heavens opened and the rain began to fall, splattering heavily against the windowpanes.

Lizzy pressed her fingers against the glass and looked out, worried about her sister. Jane would not have reached Netherfield yet. She would be getting soaked.

The rain continued all night, and it was clear that Jane would not be coming home. Mrs. Bennet was very happy indeed. Lizzy knew her mother liked it when the world followed her plans.

The next morning, breakfast was hardly over when a servant from Netherfield brought a note for Lizzy:

My dearest Lizzy,

I find myself unwell this morning, which is thanks to getting wet through yesterday, I suppose. My kind friends here will not hear of my returning home until I am better. I only have a sore throat and headache, so there is not much the matter with me.

Yours,
Jane

"I will go to see Jane," Lizzy said firmly. She was certainly worried now. Jane never complained and she could be really ill. "I can walk to Netherfield Park—it's only three miles."

"How can you be so silly?" cried her mother. "You can't possibly walk in all this mud! You will not be fit to be seen when you get there."

"I shall be very fit to see Jane, which is all I want," Lizzy replied. "I will be back by dinner."

Lizzy set off at once, crossing field after field at a fast pace. She jumped over stone walls and leaped over puddles. After the rain last night, the sky was blue and the air felt clean and fresh. By the time she reached the house at Netherfield Park her cheeks were glowing and her mother's predictions were proved right—Lizzy's shoes, stockings, and the bottom inches of her skirt were covered in mud.

She was shown into the breakfast parlor, where she was greeted with a great deal of surprise. It was clearly almost unbelievable to Mrs. Hurst and Miss Bingley that Lizzy had walked three miles in such bad weather, and all by herself.

The look they shared made it very clear that they did not approve.

Mr. Bingley jumped to his feet. "My dear Miss Bennet!" he said. "You have come to see your sister. I am glad! I am told that she did not sleep well and she has a fever."

Mr. Hurst smiled at Lizzy politely, but Mr. Darcy remained silent and serious. In truth, he was struck by how well she looked after her walk. Her eyes were bright, her cheeks pink—she looked vivid and alive.

Lizzy would have been surprised to know what Mr. Darcy's thoughts were, but she had no time to care what *anyone* thought about her. Lizzy just wanted to see Jane, and her wish was granted almost at once.

Jane was very happy to see her sister, but Lizzy realized at once that things were worse than Jane had admitted in her letter. Her fever was bad, and Jane was very weak. Lizzy did not leave her side.

Later that afternoon, Lizzy didn't know what to do. She knew that the polite thing would be to leave now and return home—a good guest did not overstay her welcome. But Lizzy didn't want to go;

she wanted very badly to stay with Jane and look after her.

Thankfully, Mr. Bingley settled the matter by insisting Lizzy stay until Jane was well again. A servant was sent to the Bennets' home to collect Lizzy's things, and Lizzy could only imagine how happy Mrs. Bennet was with the arrangement.

6.

Lizzy came down to join the others for dinner but excused herself as soon as possible to return to her sister's bedside.

Miss Bingley began insulting her as soon as she was out of the room. She said Miss Elizabeth Bennet had no style, no beauty, no manners.

Mrs. Hurst agreed with her. "She has nothing to recommend her, except being an excellent walker. I shall never forget her wild appearance this morning!" Mrs. Hurst exclaimed.

"It was silly of her to come at all!" Miss Bingley agreed. "Why must she be scampering about the country because her sister had a cold? Her hair was so untidy!"

"Yes." Mrs. Hurst nodded eagerly. "And I hope you saw her petticoat—it was six inches deep in mud, I am absolutely certain."

"I thought Miss Bennet looked remarkably well when she came into the room this morning,"

Mr. Bingley said. "Her dirty petticoat quite escaped my notice."

"You observed it, Mr. Darcy, I am sure," said Miss Bingley, "and I am inclined to think that you would not wish to see your sister Georgiana behave like that."

"Certainly not," Mr. Darcy agreed.

"Well, I think Miss Bennet's affection for her sister is very pleasing," said Mr. Bingley, but the others paid no attention to him.

"I am afraid, Mr. Darcy," Miss Bingley said in a low voice, "that this adventure must mean you no longer admire her fine eyes."

"Quite the opposite," he replied evenly. "They were brightened by the exercise."

Miss Bingley was not at all pleased with this response.

It was some time later that Lizzy returned to join her hosts. Jane was sleeping now, and Lizzy knew she had to be polite and put in an appearance. She found that they were playing cards, and Mr. Bingley invited her to join them.

"No, thank you." Lizzy smiled. "I can only stay a short while, so I will sit and read my book. Please don't let me disturb you."

The others returned to their game and Lizzy tried to focus on her book, but she was distracted by their conversation.

"Has your sister Georgiana grown much since the spring?" Miss Bingley asked Mr. Darcy. "Will she be as tall as I am?"

"I think she will," Mr. Darcy replied. "She is now about Miss Elizabeth Bennet's height, or rather taller."

"How I long to see Georgiana again!" Miss Bingley sighed. "Such a lovely girl. And so extremely accomplished for her age!"

"It is amazing to me," said Mr. Bingley, "how young ladies can have the patience to become as accomplished as they all are."

"*All* young ladies accomplished?" Miss Bingley laughed. "I don't think all of them are."

"Yes, all of them, I think," Mr. Bingley said firmly. "I never hear a young lady spoken of without hearing how accomplished she is."

Mr. Darcy frowned, replying, "I cannot boast of knowing more than half a dozen young women that are really accomplished."

Lizzy could not help interrupting here.

"Then your idea of an accomplished woman must be very strict," she said.

"Oh! Certainly," cried Miss Bingley. "A woman must have a deep knowledge of music, singing, drawing, dancing, and the modern languages to deserve the word *accomplished*. Besides all this, she must possess a certain something in her posture and manner of walking, the tone of her voice."

"An accomplished woman must have all these things," added Darcy, and there was something almost like a smile in his voice. "And to all this she must add the gift of reading extensively."

Lizzy smiled sweetly. "I am no longer surprised that you know only six accomplished women. I rather wonder now at your knowing any!"

Mr. Bingley choked on a laugh, and the card game resumed. Lizzy's eyes were fixed firmly on her book. When the game finished, Mr. Darcy sat down to write a letter.

It was not long until Miss Bingley got up and walked about the room. Lizzy noticed that her eyes strayed several times to Mr. Darcy, who was far too focused on his letter to notice.

"Miss Bennet," Miss Bingley said in a loud voice, "let me persuade you to follow my example and take a turn about the room. I assure you it is very refreshing after sitting so long in one attitude."

Lizzy was surprised but agreed to it.

Mr. Darcy looked up.

"Perhaps you would like to join us, Mr. Darcy?" Miss Bingley said with a smile that Lizzy thought was meant to be inviting.

"No, thank you." Mr. Darcy shook his head. "There are only two reasons for you to walk up and down the room together, and if I join you it will ruin both of them."

"What could he mean? Do you understand him?" Miss Bingley asked Lizzy.

"Not at all," Lizzy answered, "but I am sure he means to be hard on us. Our best way of disappointing him will be to ask nothing about it."

However, Miss Bingley was unable to disappoint Mr. Darcy in anything, and so she asked him again what he meant by ruining the reasons for walking.

"You either have secrets to discuss," Mr. Darcy said, "or you know that your figures appear to their greatest advantage when walking. If you're walking for the first reason, I would be completely in your way, and if the second reason, I can admire you much better as I sit by the fire."

"Oh! Shocking!" cried Miss Bingley. "I never heard anything so awful. How shall we punish him for such a speech?"

"It is very easy," said Lizzy with a wide smile. "Tease him—laugh at him."

"Tease him!" Miss Bingley was clearly horrified. "Laugh at *Mr. Darcy*? I would never!"

"Mr. Darcy is not to be laughed at?" Lizzy said and shook her head. "What a shame. I dearly love to laugh."

"I have always tried to avoid those weaknesses which people may laugh at," Mr. Darcy said.

"Weaknesses like vanity and pride?" Lizzy suggested.

"Yes, vanity is a weakness," Mr. Darcy agreed. "But pride? I don't think that a weakness."

Lizzy turned away to hide a smile. "Mr. Darcy has no faults then," she said.

"I have faults," Mr. Darcy replied quickly. "I can be stubborn. I am not forgiving. My good opinion, once lost, is lost forever."

"That is a failing indeed," Lizzy said seriously. "I find I cannot laugh at it."

"Do let us have a little music," cried Miss Bingley, clearly tired of a conversation that did not include her.

28

Mrs. Hurst began to play the piano, and Lizzy saw Mr. Darcy smile, though she didn't know at what. Talking to Elizabeth Bennet was becoming too enjoyable. He was not sure how he felt about that.

7.

Jane recovered quickly with her sister there to nurse her. A few days later, Jane and Lizzy were on their way home. Lizzy felt nothing but relief to be leaving. Mr. Darcy's feelings were a bit more complicated.

Life settled back into its usual pattern, until one morning Mr. Bennet cleared his throat as if about to make an important announcement.

"I hope, my dear, that you have ordered a good dinner for tonight," Mr. Bennet said to his wife, "because I have reason to expect a special guest."

"Who do you mean?" Mrs. Bennet asked in a puzzled voice.

"The person of whom I speak is a gentleman and a stranger," Mr. Bennet said. "About a month ago I received a letter. It was from my cousin, Mr. Collins. When I am dead, Mr. Collins may turn you all out of this house as soon as he pleases."

"Oh, my dear!" cried Mrs Bennet. "Please do not even mention that horrible man. You know what effect he has on my nerves!"

"Perhaps you will feel better once you hear the letter," Mr. Bennet said, and then he read the letter aloud:

Dear Sir,

I have recently been so fortunate as to be singled out by the Right Honorable Lady Catherine de Bourgh. Her wondrous generosity has moved her to give me the job of rector of her parish. I feel blessed indeed to receive even a little attention from such a superior lady.

As a clergyman, I feel it is my duty to promote the blessing of peace in all families, and so I write to you today. I am most upset that I may be the cause of unhappiness for your agreeable daughters, due to my future inheritance, and I wish to apologize for it. I also wish to assure you of my plans to make amends to them—but more of this later. If you should have no objection, I propose to visit you and your family on Monday, November 18th, by four o'clock, and shall probably trespass on your hospitality for two weeks.

I remain, dear sir, your well-wisher and friend, with respectful compliments to your lady and daughters,

William Collins

"And so at four o'clock we may expect this gentleman," said Mr. Bennet as he folded up the letter.

Lizzy could not help thinking Mr. Collins seemed a little silly in his description of Lady Catherine. "Do you think he is a sensible man, sir?" Lizzy asked her father.

"No, my dear, I think not," Mr. Bennet chuckled. "I have great hopes of finding him quite the opposite. I am impatient to see him."

Mr Collins was very punctual. He was a small man with thin brown hair and gold-rimmed spectacles, and he bowed ever so low over Mrs. Bennet's hand.

He barely stopped talking from the moment he stepped from the carriage. Nothing escaped his praise. Mr. Collins said his cousins were as beautiful as he had heard; the garden was beautiful too, along with the dining room, all of the furniture—in fact, everything Mr. Collins laid his eyes on he praised to the extreme.

At dinner Mr. Collins gushed over every dish. "This pork chop!" he exclaimed. "I have never tasted anything better! And these green beans!" He seemed almost to swoon.

Lizzy hid a giggle in her napkin.

"Tell me," Mr. Collins beamed, "which of my cousins made this delicious feast?"

Mrs. Bennet looked like an unhappy chicken ruffling her feathers. "None of my daughters work in the kitchen!" she snapped. "We are very well able to keep a good cook, thank you!"

Mr. Collins looked horrified, and his groveling apologies lasted for over fifteen minutes.

After an awkward silence, talk turned to Lady Catherine de Bourgh, a subject on which Mr. Collins had an awful lot to say.

"Does Lady Catherine live near you, sir?" Mrs. Bennet asked. Mr. Collins had just spent *another* fifteen minutes listing the delights of Lady Catherine's house, a place called Rosings Park.

"My garden is separated only by a lane from Rosings Park," Mr. Collins said proudly.

"And Lady Catherine has a daughter, I understand?" Mrs. Bennet asked.

"She does indeed." Mr. Collins nodded. "A most lovely young woman, but she suffers from poor health and so she rarely leaves home, depriving the British court of its brightest star, as I told Lady Catherine one day. Her ladyship seemed pleased with the idea, and I do like to offer such little compliments as often as possible."

"A very good idea," said Mr. Bennet, "and it is fortunate that you are so good at them. May I ask whether these compliments come to you in the moment or if you think of them beforehand?"

Mr. Collins tipped his head to one side in thought and answered very seriously. "They usually come from what is passing at the time, but I do sometimes amuse myself with planning such little elegant compliments that may be used on later occasions."

Lizzy buried her face in her napkin but could not stop a snort slipping out. She quickly covered it with a cough.

Mr. Bennet sat back in his chair, smiling. Lizzy knew he was pleased that his cousin was as silly as he had hoped.

8.

It did not take Mr. Collins long to settle in, and to make the real reason for his trip known. He now had a good house and income, and intended to marry, so who better than one of the Bennet sisters? This way the Bennets' house at Longbourn would stay in the family after Mr. Bennet's death.

So it happened that Mr. Collins began to woo Lizzy, which made her very uncomfortable. Wherever she went, Mr. Collins seemed to follow, and she was trying very hard to be polite, which made getting rid of him almost impossible.

One morning Lydia suggested a walk to the nearby village of Meryton, and Lizzy agreed quickly. She would do anything if it meant getting away from Mr. Collins.

Unfortunately, Mr. Bennet had also had enough of his cousin, and so he asked Mr. Collins to go with the girls. Mr. Collins was—of course—only too happy to oblige.

Lizzy swallowed her resentment and tried to keep a dull smile on her face as Mr. Collins droned on and on about his neighbor Lady Catherine, and how many stairs made up the grand staircase at Rosings, and what color the drapes were in the drawing room, and what she served when a humble man such as himself was invited for tea.

Kitty and Lydia made no pretense at conversation and dashed on ahead as fast as possible.

Lizzy tried to ignore Mr. Collins's droning voice and instead to focus on the birdsong, the clear blue skies, and the green hedgerows they passed on their walk. Jane made more of an effort, asking Mr. Collins gentle questions.

When they reached Meryton, Kitty and Lydia rushed up the main street, pressing their faces against the window of the dressmaker's shop.

"That hat would look wonderful on me!" Lydia exclaimed.

"You're right," Kitty agreed. Kitty was older than Lydia, but it was always clear who was in charge. Lydia tossed her dark curls approvingly.

"But look!" Lydia said. "Here comes Mr. Denny! And who is that with him? He's terribly handsome!"

Mr. Denny was an officer in the army: a smiling, friendly young man and a favorite of Lydia and Kitty. He greeted them and asked for permission to introduce his friend.

"This is Mr. Wickham," Mr Denny said. "He is about to join our regiment."

Lizzy could not help agreeing with Lydia as she bobbed into a curtsy—Mr. Wickham really was terribly handsome. His laughing gray eyes smiled down at her from under a mop of fair curls. There was a warmth and liveliness to him that Lizzy liked at once.

"I am very happy to meet you," Mr. Wickham said. "My friend Mr. Denny has told me all about the lovely Bennet sisters."

The chatter continued easily, and Mr. Wickham made them all laugh with stories of their lodgings and the men who lived there.

They were interrupted by the clatter of horses approaching. Lizzy looked up to find Mr. Bingley and Mr. Darcy riding down the street toward them.

"Miss Bennet!" Mr. Bingley exclaimed, his eyes immediately moving to Jane's face. "What a pleasant surprise to find you here. We were just on our way to Longbourn to call on you!"

Mr. Darcy seemed to be avoiding Lizzy's gaze, and in doing so his eyes fell on another—Mr. Wickham.

The way Mr. Wickham and Mr. Darcy stared at each other made Lizzy's stomach twist with shock. Mr. Wickham's cheeks had gone red, and the smile that she had been drawn to had disappeared.

Meanwhile Mr. Darcy looked like he had seen a ghost.

The next second, Wickham touched his hat as if in greeting.

There was a moment of silence. And then Mr. Darcy steered his horse around and rode away, leaving the rest of them gaping after him.

9.

It was not long before Lizzy saw Mr. Wickham again. Her aunt, Mrs. Phillips, invited the Bennets to a small party at her house, which several of the men from the regiment also attended.

Mr. Collins was being distracted by Mrs. Phillips, who seemed only too happy to listen to him raving about Lady Catherine and her mansion.

When Mr. Wickham walked into the room, Lizzy felt a bit breathless. He was even more handsome in his uniform than she remembered.

"What a horrid, wet night it is out there." Mr. Wickham grinned, shaking his head like a dog.

Lizzy smiled up at him and invited him to sit beside her. It wasn't long before they were talking like old friends about Lizzy's family and Mr. Wickham's life as a soldier.

Lizzy was enjoying the conversation very much, but there was one subject that she desperately wanted to ask about. What on earth was the meaning of that strange encounter between Mr. Wickham and Mr. Darcy?

Lizzy's good manners meant that she dared not even mention it, but her curiosity was unexpectedly relieved when Mr. Wickham began the subject himself. He asked how far Netherfield Park was from Meryton and, after receiving Lizzy's answer, asked how long Mr. Darcy had been staying there.

"About a month," said Lizzy. She paused, wanting to get to the bottom of the mystery between the two men. "He is a man of very large property in Derbyshire, I understand."

"Yes," replied Mr. Wickham. There was another awkward moment while he seemed to think about what he wanted to say. "Mr. Darcy's estate there is a noble one. I have been connected to his family for my whole life."

Lizzy's eyes widened. She was not expecting that revelation.

"I'm sure you are surprised to hear that after seeing the very cold manner of our meeting yesterday," Mr. Wickham said quickly. "Tell me, how well do you know Mr. Darcy?"

"As well as I would ever like to!" Lizzy exclaimed. "I think him very disagreeable."

"I wonder," Mr. Wickham murmured, "whether Mr. Darcy is likely to stay here much longer."

"I don't know," Lizzy admitted. "But I heard nothing about him going away when I was at Netherfield. I hope your plans will not be affected by his being here."

"Oh no! I won't be driven away by Mr. Darcy," Mr. Wickham replied. "If he wishes to avoid seeing me, *he* must go. We are not on friendly terms, and it always gives me pain to see him. His father, the late Mr. Darcy, was one of the best men that ever breathed, and I can never be in company with *this* Mr. Darcy without feeling anger and sadness. His behavior toward me has been shocking."

"But what can you mean?" Lizzy frowned at this.

Again Mr. Wickham hesitated, as if the story was a painful one and he was not sure how much to share with her.

"A military life is not what I was intended for," Mr. Wickham said finally. "The church should have been my profession—I was brought up for the church. I should at this time have been in possession of a most valuable living, if it had not been for Mr. Darcy."

"What?" Lizzy was startled out of her best behavior by this, her word ringing around them.

"Yes—the late Mr. Darcy was my godfather, and very attached to me. He left me a position and property—similar to what your cousin Mr. Collins has. But the property became vacant two years ago and Mr. Darcy gave it to someone else."

"Good heavens!" cried Lizzy. "But how could that be? How could his father's will be ignored?"

"It was not a formal situation," Mr. Wickham explained. "The late Mr. Darcy did not write it in his will, despite talking about it often. He expected his son to do the right thing, but unfortunately that did not happen."

"This is quite shocking! He deserves to be publicly disgraced," Lizzy said breathlessly.

"Some time or other Mr. Darcy will be." Mr. Wickham smiled sadly. "But not by me. I loved his father too much to disgrace his son."

This made Lizzy think Mr. Wickham handsomer than ever.

"But what can have been his motive?" Lizzy said.

"He has a complete and determined dislike of me—a dislike which I think came from jealousy.

His father's attachment to me always angered Mr. Darcy." Mr. Wickham shook his head.

"I had not thought Mr. Darcy so bad as this," Lizzy said. "But I have never liked him." She was stunned. "How can Mr. Bingley, who is truly agreeable, be friends with such a man? Do you know Mr. Bingley?"

"Not at all," Mr. Wickham said.

"He is sweet-tempered and charming," Lizzy said firmly. "He cannot know what kind of person Mr. Darcy truly is."

"Probably not." Mr. Wickham shrugged. "But Mr. Darcy can be pleasing when he chooses. He can make himself agreeable if he thinks a person is worthy of his attention. And he is a very kind and careful guardian of his sister."

"What sort of girl is Miss Darcy?" Lizzy asked.

Mr. Wickham shook his head. "I wish I could call her friendly. It gives me pain to speak ill of a Darcy. But she is too much like her brother—very, very proud. Miss Darcy is a handsome girl, about fifteen or sixteen, and highly accomplished, I understand. Since her father's death, her home has been London."

"Mr. Wickham, there you are!" called Lydia, interrupting their conversation. She was pouting and pulling at Mr. Wickham's arm. "It is very wrong of Lizzy to keep you to herself. Come and play cards with us over here!"

"I would be very happy to," Mr. Wickham replied, the easy smile back on his face as he gazed at Lizzy's sister. "That is if Miss Bennet will excuse me?"

Lizzy murmured something polite and watched Mr. Wickham be dragged away by Lydia. Then she sank into her own thoughts. Mr. Darcy was a true villain, it seemed.

10.

The next day, Lizzy told Mr. Wickham's story about Mr. Darcy to Jane. Her sister listened with shock on her face. It was almost impossible for Jane to think badly of someone. She could not believe Mr. Darcy would do anything so terrible. But she also could not believe Mr. Wickham would lie. There was nothing to be done but to somehow think well of them both.

"It is difficult indeed—it is distressing," Jane said, twisting her hands together. "One does not know what to think."

"One knows exactly what to think," Lizzy muttered. Her opinion of Mr. Darcy was now about level with that of a slug.

Seeing Jane's worried frown, Lizzy let the matter drop. There was, after all, something much more agreeable to focus on: Mr. Bingley had been easily persuaded and there was soon to be a ball at Netherfield.

*

On the evening of the ball, Lizzy arrived with her family in a state of excitement. She could admit to herself that a large part of this came from the prospect of seeing Mr. Wickham again.

Lizzy had made a special effort tonight, pinning her hair up with pretty gold combs and letting a few ringlets frame her face. Her dress was a pale cream silk, decorated with delicate gold thread that shimmered in the candlelight.

Lizzy carefully smoothed down the skirts with trembling hands and glanced around to see if she could catch sight of Mr. Wickham.

Her heart was thumping and she told herself not to be so silly . . . she hardly knew the man after all.

After her eyes had run over every soldier in a red coat, a feeling of dread settled over her. Was it possible that Mr. Wickham had not been invited because of the bad feeling between him and Mr. Darcy?

Soon Mr. Denny answered her question. He appeared, bowing and laughing, complimenting Lydia's dress while she flirted with him.

"I'm afraid Wickham had business in town and couldn't attend tonight," Mr. Denny said when Lydia asked about his friend. He caught Lizzy's eye and added in a low voice, "However, it could be that he went today to avoid a certain person."

Mr. Denny and Lizzy turned toward Mr. Darcy, who had just entered the room. Lizzy felt her rage simmer. Her disappointment about Mr. Wickham was so strong that it almost knocked her off her feet. All her excitement had been for nothing: she would not see Mr. Wickham tonight. They would not dance and laugh and talk. All because of Mr. Darcy.

The evening did not improve when Lizzy was forced to dance the first two dances with her cousin, Mr. Collins. He was serious and awkward and stepped on her toes. He got the steps wrong and spoke to Lizzy in a way that made it clear he already viewed her as being somehow his property. She was very glad when the song finished and she could curtsy and walk away.

She returned to Charlotte Lucas and was in conversation with her when she found herself suddenly addressed by Mr. Darcy. He asked her to dance, taking her so much by surprise that she accepted him without knowing what she did.

Mr. Darcy walked away again immediately, and Lizzy was left to fume.

"I dare say you will find Mr. Darcy very agreeable," Charlotte said.

"Heaven forbid!" Lizzy replied. "That would be the greatest misfortune of all! To find a man agreeable whom one is determined to hate!"

The dancing began again and Lizzy noticed the shocked looks that she got as Mr. Darcy led her out onto the dance floor. They stood for some time without speaking a word, and she thought their silence might last through the two dances.

At first she was determined that she would not be the one to break it. But after a moment she realized that the greater punishment for Mr. Darcy would be making small talk.

"It is a very nice dance," Lizzy said.

"Yes," Mr. Darcy agreed, taking her hand and leading her into a turn. His hand was warm.

They fell silent again.

"It is your turn to say something now, Mr. Darcy," Lizzy said, forcing herself to sound cheerful. "I talked about the dance, and you should now make some sort of remark on the size of the room or the number of couples."

Mr. Darcy smiled. "Do you talk by rule, then, while you are dancing?"

Lizzy stepped forward and then back, enjoying the music. "Sometimes. One must speak a little, you know. It would look odd to be silent for half an hour."

He did not answer, only smiled, and they were silent once more.

As if he was making an effort, Mr. Darcy asked if Lizzy and her sisters often walked to Meryton.

"Yes, we do," Lizzy said. "When you met us there the other day, we had just been forming a new acquaintance," she added, unable to resist the temptation of mentioning Mr. Wickham.

A flush rose to Mr. Darcy's cheeks as he said stiffly, "Mr. Wickham is blessed with such happy manners that he is always making friends— whether he is capable of holding on to them is less certain."

"He has been unlucky to lose *your* friendship," replied Lizzy, "and in a way that he is likely to suffer from all his life."

Mr. Darcy hesitated then. He was quiet, but there was something that flashed in his eyes.

"I remember hearing you once say that you hardly ever forgave people," Lizzy said quietly.

"You are very cautious, I suppose, about who you argue with?"

"I am," he said in a firm voice.

"Because those who never change their opinion must be careful to form the right opinion in the first place," Lizzy said.

"May I ask what these questions are about?" Mr. Darcy frowned.

"Merely about your character," Lizzy said. "I am trying to make it out."

"And have you succeeded?" Mr. Darcy asked. His eyes met Lizzy's and she felt a small, unexpected shiver up her spine.

She shook her head. "Not at all. I hear such different accounts of you that it puzzles me."

Lizzy said no more, and when the dance ended they parted in silence. Lizzy was flustered by the dance, and by the closeness of a man she now considered her enemy. Mr. Darcy frowned and rubbed his chest in an absent gesture. He felt Lizzy's disapproval but did not fully understand it. He did not like how much it affected him.

The rest of the ball was as disastrous as this beginning had been, from Lizzy's point of view. Mr. Collins revealed that Lady Catherine de Bourgh was Mr. Darcy's aunt and insisted on being introduced. Lizzy watched, torn between horror and amusement, as Mr. Collins rambled on and on to Mr. Darcy, who looked at him with obvious wonder. In the end, Mr. Darcy interrupted Mr. Collins, made him a slight bow, and moved another way.

But there was more embarrassment to come. Lizzy found her mother with some of the other older ladies of the party talking loudly about her Jane and Mr. Bingley. She spoke about what a fine match they were, how she expected an offer any day, and how Jane would feel at home here at Netherfield.

Everything was said clearly in the earshot of Mr. Darcy, and Lizzy caught him looking at her mother with an expression of cold dislike.

It felt to Lizzy as if her family had been trying to make a spectacle of themselves all evening, and by the end her head was aching and her spirit was weary.

11.

The next day brought fresh problems for Lizzy.

She was in the breakfast room with Kitty and her mother when Mr. Collins tapped lightly at the door.

"Mrs. Bennet," he said with a smile that showed off all of his teeth. "May I ask for the honor of a private audience with Miss Elizabeth?"

Mrs. Bennet answered instantly, before Lizzy had time to make an excuse. "Oh dear! Yes, certainly. Come, Kitty, I want you upstairs."

"No!" Lizzy yelped. "I mean . . ." she stuttered. "I beg you will not go. Mr. Collins must excuse me. He can have nothing to say to me that you should not hear. I am going away." Lizzy leaped to her feet and moved toward the door.

"Lizzy," Mrs. Bennet screeched. "I insist upon your staying and hearing Mr. Collins."

Lizzy flopped back down into her seat. There was nothing for it now but to face the worst. She knew what was coming: a proposal.

Mr. Collins was already talking.

"Almost as soon as I entered the house, I knew you would be the companion of my future life. But before I get carried away, perhaps I should state my reasons for marrying."

Lizzy winced.

Mr. Collins carried on breathlessly, "My reasons for marrying are, firstly, that I think it the right thing for a clergyman like myself to do. Second, I think it will make me happy. And third, it is the particular advice of Lady Catherine de Bourgh that I should do so—which I should perhaps have mentioned earlier. I remember the moment Lady Catherine said it to me very well. It was a Saturday. She said, 'Mr. Collins, you must marry. A clergyman like you must marry. Choose properly, choose a gentlewoman. Let her be an active, useful sort of person, not brought up high, but able to make a small income go a good way. Find such a woman as soon as you can, bring her to your home, and I will visit her.'" Mr. Collins paused. "As you can imagine, I was greatly moved by her kindness and interest. It will be the greatest blessing for you, my wife—"

Lizzy could stand it no longer.

"You are too hasty, sir," she cried. "You forget that I have made no answer. Let me do it without further loss of time. Accept my thanks for the compliment you are paying me. I am honored by your proposal, but it is impossible for me to accept."

Mr. Collins simply gave a formal wave of his hand. "I understand that it is usual with young ladies to reject the addresses of the man whom they secretly mean to accept, when he first asks them. So do not fear, my dearest Elizabeth, I shall keep asking you!"

"Oh!" cried Lizzy. "I do assure you that I am not one of those young ladies who are so daring as to risk their happiness on the chance of being asked a second time (if such young ladies there are). I am perfectly serious in my refusal. You could not make me happy, and I am convinced that I am the last woman in the world who could make you so."

Having said this, Lizzy rushed from the room as quickly as possible.

Moments later, Lizzy was summoned to the library where she found her mother and father.

"Come here, child," said her father. "I understand that Mr. Collins has made you an offer of marriage. Is it true?"

Lizzy replied that it was.

"Very well. Your mother insists that you accept it. Is it not so, Mrs. Bennet?"

"Yes, or I will never see Lizzy again." Mrs. Bennet crossed her arms.

"An unhappy choice is before you, Lizzy," Mr. Bennet said seriously. "From this day forward you must be a stranger to one of your parents. Your mother will never see you again if you do not marry Mr. Collins, and I . . ." Mr. Bennet paused here, a slight smile tugging at his lips, "will never see you again if you do."

A laugh spilled from Lizzy's lips and she threw herself into her father's arms.

Mrs. Bennet screamed and fell into a dramatic swoon against the most comfortable cushion she could find.

"Oh dear," Lizzy sighed, looking at her mother. "This is going to make life most uncomfortable."

12.

Lizzy was right, because Mrs. Bennet was still in a terrible mood the next day. She could not look at Lizzy without moaning or groaning or sobbing into a lacy handkerchief. When Charlotte Lucas came to visit, Lizzy explained what had happened, and Charlotte listened carefully.

"Lizzy!" Charlotte exclaimed. "I know you are not very fond of Mr. Collins, but he seems to be a kind man. How could you turn down that security? Just think, you could have stayed here in this house as its mistress."

"Oh, Charlotte!" Lizzy scoffed. "How can you even suggest such a thing? To be tied to such a man for the rest of my life? It would be unbearable!"

Charlotte looked like she did not agree, but she kept quiet.

"Of course, Mother is very unhappy with me," Lizzy said. "And it *is* awkward having Mr. Collins around. I thought he might leave early, but he seems determined to stay until Saturday."

"Perhaps I could invite him to visit us?" Charlotte suggested. "He seemed to get on well with my parents."

"An excellent plan!" Lizzy agreed. "But you should not have to look after my terrible relations."

"Oh, I don't mind!" Charlotte said cheerfully. "I don't think Mr. Collins is so bad."

Mr. Collins greeted the plan with almost as much relief as the Bennet sisters. Soon he and Charlotte had left, and all Lizzy had to deal with was her mother calling her ungrateful.

Lizzy and her sisters escaped for their walk to Meryton as soon as possible. Lizzy's mood lifted when they bumped into Mr. Wickham.

"We were very sorry not to see you at the ball," Lizzy said to him, a little shyly.

Mr. Wickham sighed. "I found as the time drew near that I had better not meet Mr. Darcy. I thought that to be in the same room as him, for such a long time, might be more than I could bear."

Lizzy approved of this, and for the rest of the walk she and Mr. Wickham walked side by side in conversation.

Lizzy was very aware of his smile and the warmth in his eyes. They walked, perhaps, a bit closer to each other than was proper, but they did not touch. Still, this closeness sent Lizzy's heart racing.

Even Mrs. Bennet's continued bad mood could not wipe the smile from Lizzy's face when she returned home. But then a letter arrived for Jane.

It was from Caroline Bingley and it said that Mr. Bingley and his sisters had left Netherfield. They were on their way to London, with no idea when they might return.

Lizzy took one look at the hurt in Jane's eyes and all her happiness disappeared.

"I would not mind," said Jane softly, "but it is this part of the letter that upsets me. I will read it to you."

Mr. Darcy is impatient to see his sister—
and we are just as eager to meet her again.
I think Georgiana Darcy is unmatched in
beauty, elegance, and accomplishments.
She is an extremely special young woman,
and the affection I have for her is made
stronger because of the hope I have that she
will one day be my sister.

"There," said Jane as she finished reading it out. "It is perfectly clear. Caroline is telling me that Mr. Bingley and Miss Darcy are attached and that I have been mistaken in thinking Mr. Bingley liked me in that way. She is letting me down gently. There can be no other explanation."

"Yes, there can!" Lizzy was furious. "My explanation is *very* different. Miss Bingley sees that her brother is in love with you, but she wants him to marry Miss Darcy. She follows him to town in hope of keeping him there and tries to persuade you that he does not care about you."

"Oh no!" Jane shook her head. "Caroline would not be so cruel. It must be the truth. And we must try to break it gently to our mother. She will be extremely upset to hear the Bingleys are gone away."

"Well, on that I *do* agree with you," Lizzy said unhappily. "There will be no living with Mother when she hears this."

13.

In fact, there was a greater tragedy ahead for Mrs. Bennet.

Charlotte Lucas came to call on Lizzy two days later with news of great importance. After spending the last few days together, Mr. Collins had proposed to Charlotte and she had accepted.

The possibility of Mr. Collins fancying himself in love with her friend had once occurred to Lizzy within the last day or two. But that Charlotte could encourage his affection seemed impossible, and Lizzy's shock was so great that she could not help crying out:

"Engaged to Mr. Collins! My dear Charlotte—how could you?"

There was a very awkward silence then, as Charlotte started in surprise at such a rude reaction.

"Why should you be surprised, my dear Lizzy?" Charlotte said calmly. She sat with her spine straight and her hands clasped in her lap. "Do you think it impossible that Mr. Collins should win any woman over because he did not succeed with you?"

"Of course not," Lizzy said uncomfortably. "I'm sorry. I was just surprised. Of course I am pleased for you . . . I wish you both much happiness." The words sounded small and dull.

"I understand what you are feeling," replied Charlotte. "But when you have had time to think it over, I hope you will be pleased with what I have done. I am not romantic, you know—I never was. I only want a comfortable home of my own. I am convinced that my chance of happiness with him is as good as anyone's."

"Undoubtedly," Lizzy murmured, and after another awkward pause they returned to the rest of the family. Charlotte did not stay much longer, and Lizzy was then left to think about what she had heard.

Lizzy had always felt that Charlotte's opinion of marriage was not exactly like her own, but she was surprised that Charlotte could really choose to marry without feeling any affection at all.

Needless to say, Mrs. Bennet did not take the news well. She took to her bed for several days . . . much to the relief of the rest of the household.

*

It was not long after this that the wedding between Charlotte and Mr. Collins took place.

"I hope I will hear from you very often, Lizzy," Charlotte said, squeezing her hand before the wedding ceremony.

"You certainly shall," Lizzy replied, kissing her friend lovingly on the cheek.

"And I have another favor to ask you," Charlotte went on. "Will you come and see me?" Lizzy saw uncertainty in her friend's eyes.

"Of course," Lizzy said.

"My father and Maria are coming to me in March," added Charlotte, "and I hope you will come with them."

Lizzy smiled, even though the thought of the visit filled her with dread.

The wedding took place without any fuss, and the bride and groom set off for Kent straight afterward.

Day after day passed without bringing any news of Mr. Bingley, except the rumor going around

Meryton that he would not return to Netherfield for the whole winter.

Even Lizzy began to fear that his sisters and the horrible Mr. Darcy would be successful in keeping Mr. Bingley away.

As for Jane, it was clear that she was in pain, but she chose not to talk about it—even with Lizzy.

Finally, another letter arrived from Miss Bingley and put an end to any doubt. The very first sentence said that they were happily settled in London for the winter.

Hope for Jane and Mr. Bingley was over—entirely over.

14.

In March, Lizzy was to accompany Lord Lucas and his second daughter, Maria, to visit Charlotte. As the time drew closer, Lizzy actually found herself looking forward to the change of scenery.

The journey was a long one. Lord Lucas loved to chatter, and Maria took after him in that way.

After many hours, they finally saw the parsonage where Mr. Collins and Charlotte lived. The couple appeared at the door, and the carriage stopped outside. In a moment they were all out of the carriage, exclaiming with happiness at the sight of each other. Charlotte welcomed her friend with pleasure, and Lizzy was more and more glad she had come.

They were then taken into the house, and Mr. Collins welcomed them a second time as soon as they were in the parlor. He spoke with great formality as he welcomed them to his humble abode.

They sat for a long time, admiring every article of furniture in the room and giving an account of their journey. Then Mr. Collins invited them to take a stroll in the garden, which he looked after himself.

Charlotte admitted that she encouraged this as much as possible, and Lizzy struggled not to laugh. It was clear her friend enjoyed the peace and quiet when her husband was out of the house.

They had only been staying with Charlotte for a couple of days when an invitation came to dine with Lady Catherine de Bourgh.

Mr. Collins was beside himself with joy. He clearly could not wait to show off Lady Catherine's house and his friendly relationship with her to his visitors.

Their visit to Rosings, where Lady Catherine lived, was all that was talked of the whole day and the next morning. The weather was fine the day of the visit, giving them a pleasant walk across the park. Mr. Collins spent a long time talking about how many windows the Rosings house had and what it had cost to buy so much glass.

When they arrived, they were taken to the room where Lady Catherine and her daughter were sitting.

Lord Lucas was so completely awed by the grandeur surrounding him that he had just courage enough to make a very low bow and take his seat without saying a word, and Maria, frightened almost out of her senses, sat on the edge of her chair, not knowing which way to look. Elizabeth alone was not a bit scared and gazed levelly at the women in front of her.

Lady Catherine was a tall, large woman with strong features, which might once have been handsome. Her daughter was pale and sickly, and she said very little.

They sat down to a very splendid dinner, with plate after plate of extravagant food. Mr. Collins had to stop to praise every dish, of course.

Lady Catherine had a lot of opinions, and she was very happy to share them. She asked about Charlotte's domestic concerns and gave her a great deal of advice as to the management of them all.

Lady Catherine asked Lizzy how many sisters she had and whether they were older or younger than herself. She inquired about whether any of them were likely to be married, whether they were handsome, where they had been educated, what carriage her father kept, and what had been her mother's maiden name. Lizzy answered all these questions calmly.

"Do you play and sing, Miss Bennet?" Lady Catherine asked.

"A little." Lizzy nodded.

"Oh! Then some time or other we shall be happy to hear you. Do your sisters play and sing too?" Lady Catherine demanded.

"One of them does," Lizzy replied.

"Why didn't you all learn? You should all have learned. Do you draw?" Lady Catherine's questions fell hard and fast like blows, but Lizzy did not flinch.

"No, not at all," she said.

"What, none of you?" Lady Catherine looked horrified.

"Not one of us," Lizzy said cheerfully.

"That is very strange. But I suppose you had no opportunity. Are any of your younger sisters out, Miss Bennet?" Lady Catherine's question was a demand.

"Yes, all of them are out."

"All! What, all five eligible to marry at the same time? Very odd! And you are only the second. The younger ones are out before the elder ones are married!" Lady Catherine looked horrified.

"I think it would be very unfair for younger sisters to have to sit at home because the elder may not have the means or desire to marry early," Lizzy said.

"Miss Bennet," said Lady Catherine, "you give your opinion very decidedly for so young a person."

Lizzy only nodded, and Lady Catherine continued to look shocked.

Mr. Collins chose this moment to compliment the soup.

15.

A few days after their visit to Rosings, Mr. Collins bustled into the parlor, bursting with news. Lady Catherine had some new visitors at Rosings—her nephew Colonel Fitzwilliam and his cousin ... Mr. Darcy!

Lizzy felt a pang at this. She wasn't at all sure that she wanted to see Mr. Darcy.

But it was not until almost a week after the gentlemen's arrival that they were honored with another invitation to Rosings. The invitation was accepted of course, and they joined the party in Lady Catherine's drawing room.

Mr. Darcy was as handsome as ever. He barely looked at Lizzy as he made his bow, and he sat quietly, only occasionally talking to Lady Catherine, who looked at him with pride.

Colonel Fitzwilliam was nothing like his cousin Mr. Darcy. He was a smiling, chatty man. He seated himself beside Lizzy, and they talked so happily that she saw their conversation had caught the attention of Mr. Darcy. His eyes returned to them again and again with a look of curiosity.

This curiosity was clearly shared by Colonel Fitzwilliam's aunt, Lady Catherine.

"What is that you are saying, Fitzwilliam?" Lady Catherine demanded. "What are you telling Miss Bennet? Let me hear what it is."

"We are speaking of music, madam," he said.

"Of music! I must have my share in the conversation if you are speaking of music. There are few people in England who have more true enjoyment of music than myself, or better taste. If I had ever learned to play, I should have been a great talent. How does Georgiana get on, Darcy?"

"She plays beautifully," Mr. Darcy said, and Elizabeth was startled by the transformation as a wide smile split his face, his voice warm and proud.

"I'm very glad to hear it," said Lady Catherine. "Tell her from me that she must practice a good deal."

"I assure you, madam," he replied, "that she does not need such advice. She practices constantly."

"So much the better. It cannot be done too much. I often tell young ladies that they must practice constantly. I have told Miss Bennet several times that she will never play really well unless she practices more."

Mr. Darcy winced at his aunt's rudeness and made no answer.

When coffee was over, Colonel Fitzwilliam reminded Lizzy that she had promised to play for him. She sat down at the piano, and he drew a chair near her. Lady Catherine listened to half a song and then talked loudly over the music to Mr. Darcy until he stood up and walked away.

Mr. Darcy moved closer to the piano, choosing a seat that gave him a better view of Lizzy.

"You mean to frighten me, Mr. Darcy?" Lizzy grinned, her fingers coming down on the keys. "I will not be alarmed. There is a stubbornness about me that never can bear to be frightened by others. My courage always rises at every attempt to scare me."

"I shall not say you are mistaken," Mr. Darcy replied, "because you could not *really* believe me to wish to alarm you. I think I know you well enough now to know that you find great enjoyment in sometimes sharing opinions which are not your own."

Lizzy laughed and said to Colonel Fitzwilliam, "Your cousin Mr. Darcy will teach you not to believe a word I say. I am unlucky to meet a person who knows my real character, in a part of the world where I had hoped to pass myself off with some degree of credit," she joked. "Indeed, Mr. Darcy, it is very unwise of you to point this out, because it will force me to seek revenge, and I may reveal such things that will shock your relations to hear."

"I am not afraid of you," Darcy said, smiling.

"Let me hear what you accuse him of," cried Colonel Fitzwilliam.

"You shall hear then," Lizzy said, "but prepare yourself for something very dreadful. The first time I ever saw Mr. Darcy was at a ball—and at this ball, what do you think he did? He danced only two dances, though gentlemen were scarce and more than one young lady was sitting down without a partner."

"I did not know any lady there beyond my own friends," Mr. Darcy protested.

"True, and nobody can *ever* be introduced in a ballroom." Lizzy's voice was sweetly sarcastic.

"Perhaps I should have judged better," said Mr. Darcy, "but I am not very good with strangers."

In reply, Lizzy merely said, "My fingers do not move over this instrument as well as I have seen other people play. But then I have always supposed it to be my own fault—because I will not take the trouble of practicing."

Darcy smiled straight into Lizzy's eyes, and she felt her heart leap oddly. "You are perfectly right," he said softly. "You have used your time much better than I. No one who hears you play can think anything wanting."

16.

Over the next days at the Collinses' house, Lizzy met Mr. Darcy more than once on her daily walks. And Mr. Darcy did not just say hello and then walk away, no! He actually walked *with* her. He never said a great deal, but he asked Lizzy questions about all sorts of things: her enjoyment of her visit, her love of solitary walks, and her opinion of Mr. and Mrs. Collins's happiness. He seemed perfectly happy just to listen to her talk. Lizzy did not know what to think.

One day as she walked, she bumped into Colonel Fitzwilliam. He asked if he could join her.

"Of course." Lizzy smiled. "Do you leave Kent on Saturday?"

"Yes," he said, nodding. "But Darcy has been putting it off until now. Maybe he will do so again."

"He must be anxious to see his sister," Lizzy said. "I have heard nothing but good about

Miss Darcy. She is a very great favorite with some ladies I know—Mrs. Hurst and Miss Bingley."

"I know them a little," Colonel Fitzwilliam said. "Their brother, Mr. Bingley, is a great friend of Darcy's."

"Oh yes!" said Lizzy with sarcasm. "Mr. Darcy is oddly kind to Mr. Bingley and takes very good care of him."

"Yes, I really believe Darcy does take care of him," Colonel Fitzwilliam said. "Darcy told me something on our journey here that gives me reason to think Mr. Bingley owes him a great debt."

"What do you mean?" Lizzy frowned.

"I don't know the details," Colonel Fitzwilliam replied, "but Darcy was pleased that he had saved his friend from a most foolish marriage."

Lizzy froze. "Did Mr. Darcy give you his reasons for interfering?" she asked stiffly.

"I understood that there were some very strong objections against the lady Mr. Bingley was to marry." Colonel Fitzwilliam did not seem to notice the anger in Lizzy's eyes, and the conversation turned to other things.

Lizzy smiled, but inside her heart pounded with fury.

*

Lizzy's anger had not died down later in the afternoon when she found herself alone at the parsonage. It was clearer than ever that Mr. Darcy had interfered with her sister's happiness—he had stopped Mr. Bingley from proposing to her. Lizzy's fingers curled into fists, and she found herself violently plumping a cushion when the doorbell rang.

To her utter amazement, Mr. Darcy walked into the room.

"I hope you are well," he said abruptly.

"I am," Lizzy replied with icy coldness.

Mr. Darcy did not seem to notice her tone. He sat down for a few moments and then got up and walked about the room. Lizzy was surprised but said nothing. After a silence of several minutes, Mr. Darcy came toward her. He reached out a hand and almost instantly dropped it to his side.

"In vain I have struggled," Mr. Darcy said, his words coming out in a rush. "It will not do. My feelings will not be repressed. You must allow me to tell you how ardently I admire and love you."

Lizzy's hands trembled with shock. She squeezed her fingers tightly so that he would not see them shake.

"I know I am betraying my own good name by declaring my feelings to you," Mr. Darcy continued almost angrily. "The union between our two families will be unthinkable to many; indeed it has been unthinkable to me for a long time. Yet I have found myself bewitched by you. My admiration and regard for you has only grown over time. I can no longer deny it."

Lizzy's own anger grew and grew with each of his words, shaking her from her frozen pose. "I have never desired your good opinion," she said stiffly. "I do not wish to cause anyone pain, not even you, but I am certain you will not feel badly for long."

"And this is all the reply I am to expect?" Mr. Darcy exclaimed, clearly astonished. "You are rejecting me? I might, perhaps, wish to be informed *why*."

Lizzy replied hotly, "I might as well ask why you chose to tell me that you liked me against your will, against your reason? Your proposal was little more than a list of insults against me. But I have other reasons to reject you. Do you think that anything would tempt me to accept the man who has ruined the happiness of my most beloved sister?"

Mr. Darcy's cheeks turned red.

"Can you deny that you have done it?" Lizzy challenged him.

He swallowed and replied, "I do not wish to deny that I did everything in my power to separate Bingley from your sister. I did it to protect my friend."

Lizzy gasped. Had there been a heavy object at hand she may have thrown it at him. "And what about Mr. Wickham? Will you admit how you treated him?"

"You take great interest in that gentleman," Mr. Darcy managed to say.

"You have reduced him to his present state of poverty."

"And this is your opinion of me!" cried Mr. Darcy as he walked with quick steps across the room. He stopped and turned toward her, adding, "And yet you might have overlooked these offenses if I had proposed using sweet words that hid my struggles. Did you really expect me to rejoice in the inferiority of your family?"

Lizzy felt herself growing angrier every moment, but she forced herself to remain steady, her voice cool and calm.

"You could not have made the offer of marriage in any possible way that would have tempted me to accept it," Lizzy said coldly. "From the very beginning of my acquaintance with you, your arrogance, your conceit, and your selfish scorn of the feelings of others gave me cause to dislike you. You would be the last man in the world I would ever marry."

"You have said quite enough, madam," Mr. Darcy snapped. "I understand your feelings. Forgive me for having taken up so much of your time and accept my best wishes for your health and happiness."

And with these words, Mr. Darcy left the room.

17.

The next day, Lizzy hardly knew what to do with herself. Eventually she decided to go for a walk, but carefully avoided anywhere she thought Mr. Darcy might go.

This plan was proved a failure when he appeared around a corner, walking straight toward her.

"I have been walking for some time in the hope of meeting you," Mr. Darcy said, his voice chilly and distant. "Will you do me the honor of reading this letter?" And then, with a bow, he turned and stalked away out of sight.

Lizzy looked down at the envelope in her hand. It had her name written across it in firm, neat letters. Her hands shook as she opened it.

Be not alarmed, madam, on receiving this letter. It contains no repetition of the offer of marriage that you refused yesterday.

There were two crimes that you accused me of last night—that I separated your sister and Mr. Bingley, and that I cheated Mr. Wickham out of what was rightfully his. I am writing to give you an account of my actions in both cases.

I had not been long in Hertfordshire before I saw that Bingley preferred your elder sister to any other young woman in the country. But it was not until the evening of the dance at Netherfield that I had any idea of the seriousness of his feelings. At that ball, I realized that Bingley's attentions to your sister meant there was an expectation of their marriage. From that moment, I watched my friend, and I could see that his feelings for Miss Bennet were beyond what I had ever witnessed in him. Your sister, however, seemed not to have the same feelings. She was quiet, smiling, but not obviously in love.

I told Bingley that the match was a bad one, and that I was sure that your sister did not love him. If I have wounded your sister's feelings, it was unknowingly done

and I still believe I did the right thing,
though you may not agree.

"Jane is shy!" Lizzy cried aloud, looking up from the letter that was now crushed between her fingers. "You foolish, insufferable man. Charlotte was right: we cannot win! If a woman does not make her feelings obvious, she is accused of not caring, but show too much and she is grasping or unladylike!" Impatiently, Lizzy returned to the letter.

With respect to the accusation that I injured Mr. Wickham, I must explain the whole truth of what happened.
Mr. Wickham was my father's beloved godson and my friend. My excellent father died about five years ago, and he left Mr. Wickham a legacy of one thousand pounds and asked me to help him enter the Church. Within six months, Mr. Wickham wrote to inform me that he did not want to join the Church, but that he thought it only right that he be given more money instead of the job and the house. Mr. Wickham said he would like to train to be a lawyer. I hoped,

rather than believed, it would be true and agreed. I gave him three thousand pounds more.

Being now free, Mr. Wickham's life became a wild one. For about three years I heard little of him, except that he drank and gambled his money away. He came back when the money ran out to tell me that he was ready to join the Church now and to accept the house and job that my father had wanted him to have. I hope you will agree I did the right thing in doubting Mr. Wickham's honesty in this. I refused him.

I must ask for your secrecy about what I will tell next. My sister, Georgiana, who is more than ten years younger than me, spent last summer in Ramsgate with a lady called Mrs. Yonge. It has since become clear that Mrs. Yonge and Mr. Wickham were close friends.

When Mrs. Yonge took Georgiana to Ramsgate, Mr. Wickham followed them and managed to convince Georgiana that she was in love with him. She agreed to run away with Mr. Wickham to be married in secret. She was then just fifteen years old.

Thankfully, I joined them unexpectedly a day or two before they were to run away, and Georgiana told me the truth. Perhaps you can imagine what I felt and how I acted. I could not do anything to harm my sister's reputation, but I wrote to Mr. Wickham, who left the place immediately. Mr. Wickham was certainly after my sister's fortune, but I also believe that he wanted his revenge on me.

You may wonder why I did not tell you all of this last night, but I admit I was not then composed enough to reveal the truth, painful as it is to us all. I do not know what story Mr. Wickham has told you, but this one is the whole truth. If you need proof, then you may go to Colonel Fitzwilliam, who knows everything that happened.

Yours,
Fitzwilliam Darcy

18.

Lizzy finally returned home to Longbourn, and she and Jane had much to talk about.

"Mr. Darcy proposed to you!" Jane exclaimed. "Well, I am sorry for the way he did so, but who can blame him for falling in love with you?"

"You do not blame me for refusing him?" Lizzy said.

"Blame you? Oh, no." Jane wrapped her hand around Lizzy's.

"But maybe you should blame me for thinking so well of Mr. Wickham," Lizzy said.

"Why do you mean?" Jane was puzzled.

Lizzy spoke of Mr. Darcy's letter, repeating the whole of its contents as far as they concerned Mr. Wickham.

"I do not know when I have been more shocked," said Jane. "To think Mr. Wickham is so very bad! It is almost past belief. And poor Mr. Darcy! Dear Lizzy, only consider what he must have suffered.

And poor Mr. Wickham! There is such an openness and gentleness in his manner!"

"One man has got all the goodness, and the other all the appearance of it." Lizzy sighed. "There is just enough goodness to make one good man between them. For my part, I am inclined to believe it all Mr. Darcy's."

"Lizzy," Jane said seriously, "when you first read that letter, I am sure you could not treat the matter as lightly as you do now."

"Indeed, I could not. I was very unhappy. And with no one to speak to about what I felt, no Jane to comfort me and say that I had not been so very weak and vain and nonsensical as I knew I had! Oh, how I wanted you!" Lizzy pulled her sister into a tight hug, and they did not speak for a moment.

"There is one point on which I want your advice," Lizzy said, with a bit of a sniffle. "I want to be told whether I should, or should not, tell our friends about Mr. Wickham's character."

Jane paused and then replied, "Surely there can be no need to expose Mr. Wickham so dreadfully. What is your opinion?"

"That I should not. Mr. Darcy has not authorized me to share his story. Mr. Wickham will soon be gone, and so no one needs to know what he really is. At the moment I will say nothing about it."

"You are quite right," Jane said. "To have his errors made public might ruin him forever."

When the girls went downstairs, they found Lydia leaping round the room in excitement. The regiment was leaving, but Lydia had received an invitation to accompany Mrs. Forster, the wife of the colonel of the regiment, to Brighton.

The others tried to calm Lydia down, while Lizzy drew her father aside.

"I cannot think this is a good plan," she whispered to him urgently. "Lydia is too young and unpredictable—you must not let her go!"

Her father only laughed. "Do not make yourself uneasy, my love. We shall have no peace at Longbourn if Lydia does not go to Brighton. Colonel Forster is a sensible man and will keep her out of any real mischief. She shall go."

Lizzy was forced to be content with this answer, but she could not help the feeling of uneasiness that washed over her as she looked at Lydia.

19.

Lizzy was soon distracted from worrying about what Lydia might be doing in Brighton by a letter from her aunt, Mrs. Gardiner. Lizzy was very fond of her aunt and uncle who lived in London, and the letter invited Lizzy on a trip to Derbyshire.

Four weeks passed before Mr. and Mrs. Gardiner arrived at Longbourn. They stayed one night and set off the next morning with Lizzy.

They had a wonderful time together, walking and exploring and spending long evenings talking easily. Lizzy was quite happy. Near the end of their trip, the three travelers headed to the little town of Lambton, which had been Mrs. Gardiner's childhood home. And Lizzy discovered that Mr. Darcy's home, Pemberley, was situated within five miles of Lambton.

It would not be very out of their way to visit the place, and Mr. and Mrs. Gardiner asked Lizzy if she would like to do so.

Lizzy was distressed. She felt that she had no business at Pemberley. The possibility of meeting Mr. Darcy also occurred to her. It would be dreadful! She blushed at the very idea, but then her aunt mentioned that none of the Darcy family was at Pemberley just at the moment.

Now that was intriguing. She could not help but wonder what Mr. Darcy's grand home would actually be like. In the end, curiosity won out and Lizzy agreed to the visit.

As they drove along in the open carriage, they passed through woodlands, silvery trees shining in the glowing light of late spring. It was beautiful. Lizzy's mind was too full to talk, but she saw and admired everything.

They gradually climbed a hill and emerged at the top. Lizzy's breath caught at the view before them. Pemberley was situated on the opposite side of a valley, where the house rose, large and handsome, behind a pool of twinkling blue water. Banks of wildflowers tumbled down to meet the water. Lizzy had never seen a place so lovely.

They descended the hill, crossed the bridge, and drove to the door. While they waited for the housekeeper to meet them, Lizzy felt another moment of panic. What if her aunt had been wrong? What if Mr. Darcy should appear?

But he did not. The housekeeper arrived instead, and she was a cheerful woman, very happy to show off the house to visitors. In the dining room, Lizzy moved to the window to enjoy the view once more. As they passed into other rooms, every window showed beautiful views of the lake, the hills, the gardens. The rooms too were beautiful, elegant, and comfortable.

"And of this place I could have been mistress!" Lizzy whispered to herself in a daze.

After their tour of the house ended, the three of them walked outside into the golden sunshine. Lizzy wandered a little way ahead, and down by the water she turned to look back, one last time, at the house.

It was there, while knee-deep in wildflowers, that she found herself suddenly and unexpectedly face-to-face with Mr. Darcy.

20.

Their eyes met, and Lizzy felt a wave of heat rush to her face. He stared, and for a moment seemed frozen in shock.

"Miss Bennet!" he exclaimed.

"Mr. Darcy." Lizzy's voice was very low as she bobbed an awkward curtsy. She noticed that he looked less polished than usual, his boots muddy, his dark hair falling across his forehead. She had an unexpected urge to brush that hair back, and she curled her fingers.

"Your . . . your family is well?" Mr. Darcy said, falling back on his good manners.

"They are very well," Lizzy replied.

"Good," Mr. Darcy said. "Good."

They stood in silence for a long moment. Lizzy felt embarrassment flooding her down to her toes.

"You will excuse me." Mr. Darcy bowed stiffly, turned, and hurried away.

"Was that Mr. Darcy?" Lizzy's aunt asked when she and her uncle reached her.

"We must go!" gasped Lizzy. "To be discovered like this! It is terrible, terrible!"

Her aunt and uncle did not understand how truly awful the situation was, and Lizzy could hardly explain it to them. Her relatives did not hurry along as she would like but continued their walk along the banks of the water.

Lizzy thought that Mr. Darcy had run away to avoid her, so she was shocked once more when only minutes later he returned. His hair was neatly brushed, his boots spotless.

Mr. Darcy bowed to Lizzy, then asked, "Would you do me the honor of introducing me to your friends?"

"My aunt and uncle," Lizzy said, gesturing them over. "Mr. and Mrs. Gardiner." Lizzy waited for Darcy to be cold and rude, knowing how little he cared for her family.

Instead he smiled.

It was a very good smile.

Soon the four of them were walking the grounds, Mr. Darcy pointing out things he thought Lizzy might like. He got drawn into a deep conversation with Mr. Gardiner about fishing,

Mr. Darcy inviting him to come and fish in the lake any time he liked.

Mrs. Gardiner gave Lizzy a look of wonder as they walked arm in arm. Lizzy said nothing, but she felt something warm in her chest that she pushed away.

Soon Mrs. Gardiner joined her husband, and Mr. Darcy and Lizzy were left to walk together.

"I must apologize for being here," Lizzy began quickly. "We had no idea you would be here, or I would never, never have presumed—"

Mr. Darcy cut her off with a wave of his hand. "I am glad you are here," he said simply, and the warm feeling rose in Lizzy again, the one she was trying hard to ignore.

"Business brought me back to Pemberley early," Mr. Darcy continued, "but tomorrow I will be joined by the rest of my party. Among them are Mr. Bingley and his sisters."

Lizzy answered only with a slight bow. Her thoughts leaped back to the time when Mr. Bingley's name had last been mentioned between her and Mr. Darcy.

"There is also one other person in the party," he continued after a pause, "who wishes to be known to you—my sister. Will you allow me to introduce her to you during your stay at Lambton?"

"Of course," Lizzy said, surprised. "I would very much like to meet her."

Mr. Darcy looked pleased by her response.

At the end of their walk, Lizzy and Mr. Darcy parted with utmost politeness. Mr. Darcy helped the ladies into the carriage, and when it drove off, Lizzy watched him walking slowly toward the house.

21.

A few days later, Lizzy and her aunt and uncle were invited to dine at Pemberley. Lizzy was surprised to find herself so excited about the idea, but she tried to put it out of her mind as she got dressed that morning. There was no reason for her to be so pleased to return to Pemberley. She told herself she was just looking forward to seeing Mr. Bingley again.

It was another sunny day, and Lizzy was just preparing to go for a walk with her aunt and uncle when the mail arrived.

"Here are two letters from Jane!" Lizzy exclaimed. "I was wondering why I had not heard from her, but this first one must have been delayed."

Lizzy sat down and opened the first letter. It had been written five days ago. The beginning contained an account of all their parties and engagements, but then suddenly Jane's writing changed, becoming more messy, as if written in a hurry.

Since writing the above, dearest Lizzy, something most unexpected and serious has happened. What I have to say relates to poor Lydia. A message came at twelve last night, from Colonel Forster, to inform us that she was gone off to Scotland with one of his officers ... with Mr. Wickham! Imagine our surprise. I am very, very sorry, with all we know of him. But I am willing to hope for the best, and that Mr. Wickham's character has been misunderstood. Lydia left a short letter informing the Forsters that she and Mr. Wickham had run away to get married. I must stop writing, for I cannot be long from our poor mother.

Without waiting, Lizzy tore anxiously into the second letter.

Dear Lizzy,

By this time, my dearest sister, you have received my hurried letter. I'm afraid

I have more bad news for you. We now think the marriage between Mr. Wickham and Lydia has not taken place. They are together alone, unmarried, and have been gone for several days!

Some of the officers said that Wickham never meant to go to Scotland, or to marry Lydia at all! Colonel Forster has discovered they were in fact headed toward London.

Our distress, my dear Lizzy, is very great. Father and Mother believe the worst, that Mr. Wickham has ruined our sister, but I cannot think so badly of him. Perhaps he simply wanted to get married in London?

Father is going to London with Colonel Forster, to try to find Lydia and Mr. Wickham. I think they would like our uncle to go with them. I hope you will all be able to come home as soon as possible.

Yours,
Jane

"Oh! Where is my uncle?" cried Lizzy, darting from her seat.

As she reached the door it was opened by a servant, and Mr. Darcy appeared. Her pale face and the tears in her eyes sent a feeling of panic through him. He felt a strong desire to wrap her in his arms, and only just stopped himself from doing so.

"I beg your pardon, but I must leave you," Lizzy babbled. "I must find my uncle Mr. Gardiner this moment."

"Good God! What is the matter?" cried Mr. Darcy, with more feeling than politeness. Then, recollecting himself, he added, "Let me or let the servant go after Mr. and Mrs. Gardiner. You are not well, Lizzy. You cannot go yourself."

Lizzy hesitated, but her knees trembled under her, and Mr. Darcy was already calling the servant back, instructing her to go after Mr. and Mrs. Gardiner.

Lizzy sank into the chair.

"Let me call your maid," Mr. Darcy said. "Is there nothing I can get you?" He stood in front of her, worry in his eyes.

"No, thank you," she replied, trying to calm down. "I'm quite well. I am only distressed by some dreadful news I have just received from home."

The tears Lizzy had been holding in burst from her then, and for a few minutes she could not speak. Mr. Darcy reached for her hand and squeezed it gently.

"I have just had a letter from Jane," Lizzy sobbed. "My younger sister has left all her friends and has eloped with ... with Mr. Wickham. They are gone off together from Brighton. You know him too well to doubt the rest. Lydia has no money, no connections, nothing that can tempt him to marry her—she is lost forever, her reputation ruined."

Mr. Darcy's eyes widened and his face paled. He let go of her hand, and she felt the loss of his touch.

"When I consider that I might have prevented it!" Lizzy went on, her voice angry. "Had I explained some part of what Mr. Wickham was like to my family, this could not have happened. But it is too late now."

"I am grieved indeed," said Mr. Darcy, "grieved and shocked. But is it absolutely certain?"

"Oh yes! They left Brighton together on Sunday night and were traced to London." Lizzy had control of herself now.

"And what has been done to find her?" Mr. Darcy asked.

"My father is gone to London, and Jane has written to beg my uncle's help. We shall be off, I hope, in half an hour. But how are they even to be discovered?"

Mr. Darcy shook his head. He seemed not to hear her and was walking up and down the room.

"I am sorry, very sorry for this," Mr. Darcy said finally. "I wish . . . well, I will not torment you with my wishes. I fear this unfortunate affair will prevent my sister from having the pleasure of seeing you at Pemberley tonight."

"Oh yes. Be so kind as to apologize for us to Miss Darcy," Lizzy said. "Say that urgent business calls us home immediately."

Mr. Darcy bowed once more and left the room in long, hurried strides.

I will never see him again, Lizzy thought.

22.

They made their way to Longbourn without delay. When they arrived, Lizzy jumped out of the carriage and ran into Jane's arms.

"Is Father in London? Have you heard from him?" Lizzy asked.

"Yes." Jane nodded. "He wrote me a few lines on Wednesday to say that he had arrived safely. He added that he would not write again until he had news."

They went in to see Mrs. Bennet. She was keeping to her bedroom, weeping loudly and calling Mr. Wickham a villain and blaming everyone she could think of for this disaster.

"Hush, sister," Mr. Gardiner said. "I will be in London tomorrow. In a few days, we may have some news of them."

"Oh! My dear brother," replied Mrs. Bennet, "that is exactly what I wish for. And when you get to town, you will find them and if they are not married already, make them marry. And, above all, keep Mr. Bennet from fighting. Tell him what a dreadful state I am in, that I have such tremblings, such flutterings, that I can get no rest. And tell my dear Lydia not to choose her wedding clothes until she has seen me, because she does not know the best places to shop."

The days passed without news, and then Mr. Bennet came home. He looked almost gray with worry. Nothing had been found, and Mr. Gardiner had stayed behind in London to keep looking.

Two days after Mr. Bennet's return, he got a letter. As soon as Jane and Lizzy heard about this, they rushed to find their father. He was walking in the garden.

"Oh, Papa, what news? Is the letter from our uncle?" Lizzy gasped when she reached him.

"Yes," her father said.

"Well?" Lizzy was impatient. "What news does it bring—good or bad?"

"What good news could there be?" her father asked, removing the letter from his pocket. "But perhaps you would like to read it."

Lizzy took it from him.

"Read it out loud," said their father, "for I hardly know myself what it is about."

"My dear brother," Lizzy read. "At last I am able to send you some news of my niece, and I hope it will make you happy. Soon after you left me on Saturday, I found out where Lydia and Mr. Wickham were. I have seen them both. They are not married, but I hope it will not be long before they are, if you are willing to agree to the arrangements which I have made.

"Mr. Wickham's circumstances are not so hopeless as they are generally believed to be. There will be some money left, even when all his debts are paid. Send back your answer as fast as you can. We think it best that they get married here. I shall write again soon."

When she had finished, Lizzy cried, "Is it possible? Can it be possible that he will marry her?"

"Mr. Wickham is not so terrible, then, as we thought him," said Jane.

"And may I ask what arrangements my uncle made?" said Lizzy.

Her father handed her another sheet of paper. It contained a list of Mr. Wickham's bills to be paid, and a small amount of money for Lydia.

Lizzy read this wide-eyed.

"There is nothing else to be done but for them to marry." Mr. Bennet sighed. "But there are two things that I want very much to know: one is how much money your uncle has promised to Wickham to bring about the marriage. The other is how I am ever to repay him."

"Money! My uncle!" cried Jane. "What do you mean?"

"I mean that no man in his senses would marry Lydia when she has no fortune."

"That is very true," said Lizzy. "Oh! It must be my uncle! A generous, good man. But a small amount of money could not fix this."

"No," said her father. "Wickham's a fool if he marries Lydia for anything less than ten thousand pounds."

"Ten thousand pounds!" Lizzy gasped, and Jane turned white. "Heaven forbid! How is such a sum to be repaid?"

Mr. Bennet made no answer. They walked back in silence to the house, each deep in thought.

Inside, the girls decided it was time to break the news to their mother.

When she heard what had happened, Mrs. Bennet could hardly contain herself.

"My dear, dear Lydia!" she cried. "This is delightful indeed! She will be married at sixteen! My good, kind brother to have arranged this! I knew he would manage everything! How I long to see her, and to see dear Mr. Wickham too! But the clothes, the wedding clothes! I will write to my sister Mrs. Gardiner about them directly. Lizzy, my dear, run down to your father and ask him how much he will give her. My dear, dear Lydia! How merry we shall be together when we meet!"

23.

Jane and Lizzy dreaded Lydia and Mr. Wickham's return to Longbourn. The family gathered together to meet the newly married couple. Mrs. Bennet was all smiles as the carriage drove up to the door. Her husband looked serious. Lizzy and her sisters were alarmed, anxious, uneasy.

Lydia tumbled from the carriage into Mrs. Bennet's arms. The two of them screamed happily at each other, while Mr. Wickham smiled, as handsome and charming as ever.

Mr. Bennet hardly said a word. Lizzy and Jane were both shocked by how at ease Lydia and Mr. Wickham were. Lydia was still Lydia: untamed, shameless, wild, noisy, and fearless.

"Well, Mama," Lydia said later, when the women were alone, "and what do you think of my husband? Is he not a charming man? I am sure my sisters must all envy me. They must all go to Brighton. That is the place to get husbands."

"I do not much like your way of getting husbands," Lizzy said quietly.

One morning, soon after the new couple's arrival, Lydia was sitting with Jane and Lizzy when she said, "Lizzy, I never told you about my wedding. You were not there when I told Mama and the others all about it. Aren't you curious to hear about it?"

"Not really," replied Lizzy, her nose buried firmly in her book.

"You are so strange!" Lydia giggled. "But I must tell you how it went. Mr. Wickham and I were married at St. Clement's, and it was settled that we should all be there by eleven o'clock. My uncle and aunt and I were to go together, and the others were to meet us at the church.

"Well, just as the carriage came to the door, my uncle was called away upon business. I was so frightened I did not know what to do, for my uncle was to give me away. Luckily, he came back again in ten minutes' time, and then we all set out." Lydia tipped her head to one side. "I did think afterward that it would have been all right, because Mr. Darcy could have walked me down the aisle."

"Mr. Darcy was there?" said Lizzy, amazed.

"Oh yes." Lydia stopped suddenly and clapped her hand to her mouth. "But gracious me! I quite forgot! I promised Darcy to keep it a secret!"

Lydia laughed and would say no more. Questions gnawed at Lizzy. As soon as she could, she sent off a letter to her aunt asking for an explanation.

The answer to her letter came in two days.

My dear niece,

I have just received your letter and was surprised by it. I thought you knew the reasons behind Mr. Darcy's actions, but if you really do not know the whole story, then I will happily tell you.

When your uncle was in London, Mr. Darcy called and spent several hours with him. Mr. Darcy came to tell your uncle that he had found out where your sister and Mr. Wickham were and that he had talked with them both. I understand that Mr. Darcy left Derbyshire only one day after ourselves.

Mr. Darcy said that it was his fault that Mr. Wickham had been allowed to trick your sister, because his pride had stopped him from sharing the story of Mr. Wickham's true character.

He found Lydia and Mr. Wickham, and he paid Mr. Wickham a good deal of money. Mr. Darcy insisted the fault was his, so it was for him to fix, and your uncle had to accept this as well as the credit!

When all this was settled, Mr. Darcy returned again to his friends, who were still staying at Pemberley. But it was agreed that Mr. Darcy would come to London for the wedding and to deal with all the money issues.

As Lydia informed you, Mr. Darcy attended the wedding. He also dined with us the next day. Will you be angry with me, my dear Lizzy, if I say how very much I like him?

Yours, very sincerely,
M. Gardiner

24.

Lizzy turned Mr. Darcy's actions over in her mind. Why had he helped Lydia—helped their family? Was her aunt hinting that Mr. Darcy still had feelings for Lizzy? And how had she misjudged him so badly?

Lydia and Mr. Wickham left for their new home in the north, and the days passed slowly. Lizzy was restless—she did not know what to do with herself.

Finally, something happened to break through the dullness of the days. They heard that the housekeeper at Netherfield had received orders to prepare for the arrival of Mr. Bingley, who was coming down in a day or two.

Jane had gone first white then pink when she heard the news.

"I assure you," she said to Lizzy later, "that the news gives me neither pleasure nor pain."

Lizzy was sure her sister did not mean this, but she did not say anything to upset her further.

The day came when Mr. Bingley arrived. He rode
to Longbourn that very afternoon. Mrs. Bennet saw
him first, from her dressing-room window, as he
came toward the house.

"Girls! Girls!" Mrs. Bennet shrieked.

They rushed to the window.

"There is another gentleman with him," said
Mary.

"It looks just like that man that used to be with
him before. That tall, proud man." Kitty pressed
her fingers to the glass.

Lizzy felt her knees begin to shake and sat
down with a bump.

"Mr. Darcy!" Mrs. Bennet said, curling her lip.
"Well, any friend of Mr. Bingley's will always be
welcome here, but I must say that I hate the very
sight of him."

Lizzy closed her eyes. She had kept the secret
of her aunt's letter, even from Jane. Her family
did not know Mr. Darcy's true character. This was
going to be terrible.

The door opened and the two men came in.

Lizzy said as little as possible. She glanced at
Mr. Darcy. He looked serious and remained silent.

He was different at Pemberley, Lizzy realized, more relaxed and happy.

"I hope your sister is well," Lizzy said to him. It was all she could manage.

"It is a long time, Mr. Bingley, since you went away," said Mrs. Bennet.

Mr. Bingley agreed.

"I began to be afraid you would never come back again," Mrs. Bennet went on. "A great many changes have happened in the neighborhood since you went away. Miss Lucas is married and settled. And one of my own daughters. I suppose you have heard of it."

"I did indeed," Mr. Bingley said. "Many congratulations."

Lizzy dared not lift up her eyes, but she longed to see Mr. Darcy's face.

"It is a delightful thing, to have a daughter well married," continued her mother. "But we are so happy to have you back, Mr. Bingley."

Mrs. Bennet went on for several more minutes. She was full of praise for Mr. Bingley but cold and rude to Mr. Darcy. Lizzy wanted to disappear.

As soon as the gentlemen left, Lizzy walked out of the room. She needed to be alone, to think. Why had Mr. Darcy come at all—if he was only going to sit in stiff silence and make no effort to talk to her?

Finally, Lizzy was joined by Jane.

"Now that this first meeting is over," Jane said, "I feel perfectly easy. I am glad Mr. Bingley will dine here on Tuesday. Then everyone will see we are just polite with each other."

"Oh yes, just polite!" Lizzy laughed. "Oh, Jane, take care."

"My dear Lizzy, you cannot think me so weak as to be in danger now?" Jane frowned.

Lizzy's eyes twinkled. "I think you are in very great danger of making Mr. Bingley as much in love with you as ever."

25.

Mr. Bingley did not wait until Tuesday.

The next morning, Mrs. Bennet ran to her daughter's room in her dressing gown and with her hair half finished.

"My dear Jane," she cried out, "hurry down. Mr. Bingley is come. Make haste, make haste. Get your gown on!"

Jane's eyes widened as they met Lizzy's in the mirror. Lizzy squeezed her sister's hand.

They all met for tea in the sitting room. The air was thick with tension. Mr. Bingley seemed hardly able to keep still.

Mr. Bennet escaped to his library as soon as he could, and Mary excused herself to go and practice her piano.

Mrs. Bennet sat looking and winking at Lizzy and Kitty for a considerable time. Lizzy pretended not to notice her. When Kitty finally did, she said with innocence, "What is the matter, Mama? Why do you keep winking at me?"

"Wink at you! I did not wink at you," Mrs. Bennet said loudly.

Kitty only looked more confused.

Mrs. Bennet gave up her hints and got to her feet.

"Come here, my love, I want to speak to you," Mrs. Bennet said, and she hauled Kitty out of the room.

Jane looked at Lizzy with desperation. Lizzy could read that look. It said, don't leave me.

A few minutes later, Mrs. Bennet half opened the door and called out, "Lizzy, my dear, I want to speak with you."

There was nothing for Lizzy to do but go. But she refused to go far, remaining quietly in the hall.

As soon as her mother and Kitty had left, Lizzy crept back into the sitting room.

She stopped suddenly in the doorway, surprised by the sight of Jane and Mr. Bingley standing before the fireplace, their hands clasped tightly together. Lizzy took one look at Jane's joyful face and knew what had happened. Bingley had proposed.

Mr. Bingley grinned, bowed, and whispered something in Jane's ear. Jane nodded and Mr. Bingley left the room.

Lizzy and Jane raced toward each other, falling into each other's arms, laughing and crying and talking all at once.

"'It's too much!" Jane beamed. "I must go to Mother," she cried. "Mr. Bingley is gone to speak to Father already. Oh, Lizzy! To know that this news will give such pleasure to all my dear family!"

It was a day of delight to them all, and Jane glowed with happiness. Mrs. Bennet talked to Bingley of nothing else but her own joy for at least half an hour. When Mr. Bennet joined them for lunch, his voice and manner showed how happy he was.

"Jane, I congratulate you," Mr. Bennet said later. "You will be a very happy woman."

Jane went to him and kissed him.

"You are a good girl," he said. "I have not a doubt you will do very well together. You are both so easygoing that nothing will ever be decided, and so generous that you will always exceed your income."

"Exceed their income! My dear Mr. Bennet," cried his wife, "what are you talking of? Why, Mr. Bingley is a very rich man. Oh, my dear, dear Jane, I am so happy! I am sure I shan't get a wink of sleep tonight. I was sure you could not be so beautiful for nothing! Oh! He is the handsomest young man that ever was seen!"

26.

It was about a week after Jane's engagement to Mr. Bingley that Lizzy received a very surprising visitor: Lady Catherine de Bourgh.

She entered the room like a thundercloud and sat down without saying a word.

After sitting for a moment in silence, Lady Catherine said very stiffly to Lizzy, "I hope you are well, Miss Bennet."

Another silence fell. What on earth was she doing here? Lizzy wondered.

"Miss Bennet," Lady Catherine said at last, "there seems to be a pretty patch of wilderness on one side of your lawn. I should be glad to take a walk, if you will favor me with your company." Lady Catherine was already on her feet and Lizzy had no choice but to follow.

As soon as they reached the garden, Lady Catherine swung around to face Lizzy. "You know why I am here," she said.

Lizzy shook her head, startled. "No, madam," she said truthfully. "I have not the faintest idea."

"Miss Bennet," replied Lady Catherine, in an angry tone, "you should know that I am not to be trifled with. A report of a most alarming nature reached me two days ago. I was told that you were soon to be engaged to my nephew, Mr. Darcy. I know it must be a scandalous falsehood, but I set off to meet you immediately so that I might make my feelings about it known to you."

"I wonder why you took the trouble of coming so far if you believed it could not be true," Lizzy said stiffly, her heart racing.

"I came to hear you tell me at once that it is not true." Lady Catherine's words cracked like a whip.

Lizzy said nothing, only met Lady Catherine's glare with one of her own.

"Miss Bennet, I insist on being satisfied," Lady Catherine snapped. "Has my nephew, Mr. Darcy, made you an offer of marriage?"

"Your ladyship has declared it to be impossible," Lizzy replied.

"Because it should be!" Lady Catherine's voice rose. "If you married my nephew, you would be despised by everyone connected with him; your name would never even be mentioned by any of us."

"These are heavy misfortunes," Lizzy said through gritted teeth. "But the wife of Mr. Darcy would have much to make up for it."

"You obstinate, headstrong girl!" Lady Catherine exclaimed. "Tell me once and for all, are you engaged to Mr. Darcy?"

There was a moment of silence.

"I am not," Lizzy said finally.

Lady Catherine seemed pleased. "And will you promise me never to enter into such an engagement?"

"I will make no promise of the kind," Lizzy said quickly, and with that she turned and began to walk away.

"Not so hasty, if you please!" Lady Catherine hurried after her. "I have more to say. Do you think I don't know the story about your sister and Mr. Wickham? To marry into such a family! What are you thinking? Are the shades of Pemberley to be thus polluted?"

"Lady Catherine, I have nothing further to say." Lizzy came to a halt by her Ladyship's waiting carriage. "Any decisions I make about my life will be based upon the happiness of myself and those I care about. I will certainly not consider the opinion of anyone so wholly unconnected to me as you are."

With a cry of frustration, Lady Catherine climbed into her carriage. "I take no leave of you, Miss Bennet. I send no compliments to your mother. You deserve no such attention. I am most seriously displeased."

The carriage door shut with a click and the horses began to pull it away.

27.

Without really being aware of it, Lizzy knew deep down that Mr. Darcy would come. And sure enough, the next day he and Mr. Bingley arrived at Longbourn together, inviting the Bennet sisters to go for a walk. All but Mary agreed to the plan.

Mr. Bingley and Jane soon dawdled behind Lizzy, Kitty, and Mr. Darcy.

Very little was said until Kitty suggested she might run ahead to call on Maria Lucas.

Lizzy and Mr. Darcy were finally alone.

Lizzy took a deep breath. "Mr. Darcy, I am a very selfish creature. I know you wanted it kept a secret, but I can no longer help thanking you for your kindness to my poor sister. I have been most anxious to tell you how grateful I am. If the rest of my family knew the truth, then they would be grateful too."

Mr. Darcy looked uncertain for a moment, pausing his walk and frowning down at his hands.

"If you will thank me," he said finally in a low voice, "let it be for yourself alone. As much as I respect your family, I believe I thought only of you."

Lizzy was too embarrassed to say a word. In the silence that followed, she could hear her heart hammering like a drum.

The silence was about to become unbearable when Mr. Darcy broke it.

"You are too generous to trifle with me," he said. "If your feelings toward me are still what they were last March, tell me so at once. My affections and wishes are unchanged, but one word from you will silence me on this subject forever."

They stood in the middle of the path. He was looking down at Lizzy with such warmth in his brown eyes that she had to look away.

"My feelings . . ." she began but paused, knowing that she needed to choose the right words. "My feelings are the opposite of what they were. I—I admire you, and I love you. Ardently." She said the last word with a twinkling smile.

A matching smile split Darcy's face, one that Lizzy had never seen before, one that made his handsomeness almost blinding.

They walked on, without knowing in what direction. There was too much to be thought and felt and said to pay attention to anything else.

"It was my aunt's visit that taught me to hope," Mr. Darcy said. "I knew that if you had decided not to marry me you would have said so to Lady Catherine, frankly and openly."

Lizzy blushed and laughed as she replied, "Yes, you know enough of my frankness to believe me capable of that. After I'd abused you so awfully to your face, I would have no problem in abusing you to all your relations."

"What did you say of me that I did not deserve?" Mr. Darcy said. "I behaved horribly. The things I said . . ." He trailed away.

Lizzy covered his hand with her own. His fingers closed over hers as if they would never let go. "We both said a lot of things I'm sure we regret," Lizzy said quietly. "I know I do."

"I have been a selfish being all my life," Darcy said seriously. "I was spoiled by my parents, who allowed and encouraged me to be selfish. They were good themselves but taught me to care for none beyond my own family circle, to think meanly of all the rest of the world. I might still have been like that but for you, dearest, loveliest Elizabeth!"

Lizzy squeezed his hand then, tears in her eyes. "I am almost afraid of asking what you thought of me when we met at Pemberley. You were angry with me for going?" she asked, changing the subject.

"No indeed, I felt nothing but surprise, and then gladness that you were there," Darcy said simply.

"Your surprise could not be greater than mine." Lizzy grinned at him. "I had not expected you to be so friendly after the way we had parted."

"When I saw you, I wanted to show you that we could be friends," Mr. Darcy said. "I convinced myself that was what I wanted." He smiled. "I believe it was about half an hour after I had seen you that I realized I was still in love with you."

There was nothing for Lizzy to do but lift her face for Darcy's kiss that came then—a perfect, burning kiss that told him everything in her heart.

28.

Lizzy's family was much surprised at her announcement, but they were quickly happy to welcome Mr. Darcy, who smiled at Lizzy with such love in his eyes that no one could deny it. And his fortune did much to make Mr. Darcy the picture of perfection in Mrs. Bennet's eyes.

"I always liked Mr. Darcy," she confided to anyone who would listen. "It was clear from the start that he was taken by my Lizzy, and that, I think, shows great strength of character."

"*Was* it clear from the start?" Lizzy asked Mr. Darcy teasingly during one of their rare moments alone. "How did you begin to fall in love with me?"

"I cannot determine the hour, or the spot, or the look, or the words," he replied, laughing. "I was in love before I knew it."

"My beauty did not win you over," Lizzy mused. "And as for my manners . . . well, I was almost always quite rude to you. Now tell the truth, did you admire me for my boldness?"

"For the liveliness of your mind, I did," he said smoothly.

"Oh, very nice!" Lizzy kissed his cheek. "But you may as well call it boldness. The fact is that you were sick of people being polite and groveling to you. I interested you because I was so unlike them. I think that perfectly reasonable. To be sure, you saw no actual good in me—but nobody thinks of that when they fall in love."

"Was there no good in your affectionate behavior to Jane while she was ill at Netherfield?" Mr. Darcy asked.

"Dearest Jane! Who could have done less for her?" Lizzy sighed. "But praise me for it by all means. As a good husband you are to exaggerate my good qualities as much as possible. Perhaps you can even convince Lady Catherine of them. Shall you ever have the courage to let her know about our engagement?"

"I am more likely to want more time than courage, Lizzy," Mr. Darcy said. "But it should be done, and if you will give me a sheet of paper, I shall do it now."

"And if I did not have a letter to write myself, I might sit by you and admire the evenness of your writing," Lizzy replied. "But I have an aunt too, who must not be neglected."

The letter that Lizzy wrote to her aunt was long and full of exclamation marks. There was much to share and much to celebrate, but it is the end of this letter that is also a most fitting end for this story.

You must write again very soon, and praise Mr. Darcy a great deal more than you did in your last letter. I thank you, again and again, for taking me to Pemberley! How could I be so silly as to wish to avoid it? I am the happiest creature in the world! Perhaps other people have said so before, but it could not have been true. I am happier even than Jane—she only smiles, but I laugh. You are to come to Pemberley at Christmas. Mr. Darcy sends you all the love in the world that he can spare from me.

Your loving niece,
Elizabeth

Get lost in timeless classic retellings.

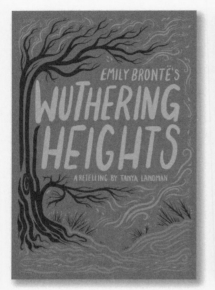

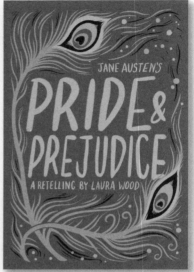

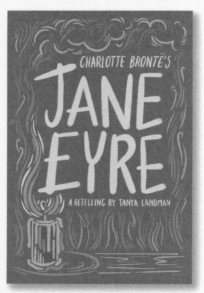

EVERYONE CAN BE A READER

Our books are tested
for children and young people by
children and young people.

Thanks to everyone who consulted on
a manuscript for their time and effort in
helping us to make our books better
for our readers.